My Loose Thread

My Loose Thread Dennis Cooper

CANONGATE

The author is eternally grateful to Joel Westendorf, Amy Gerstler, Ira Silverberg, Jamie Byng, Colin McLear, Sue De Beer, Rob Weisbach, and Terrence Malick.

First published simultaneously in Great Britain and
the United States of America in 2002 by Canongate Books Ltd,
14 High Street,
Edinburgh EH1 1TE

10 9 8 7 6 5 4 3 2 1

British Library Cataloguing-in-Publication Data
A catalogue record for this book is available on
request from the British Library

ISBN 1 84195 274 5

Typeset by Palimpsest Book Production Limited,
Polmont, Stirlingshire
Printed and bound by
R.R. Donnelley, USA

www.canongate.net

for Aspen Michael Taylor

1.

We're parked in the hills overlooking the town. It's dusk, or maybe not. Down there, they can't see like they did. It'll take them a while to figure that out. When they do, it'll look great from here, I guess. It's his thing.

'Nice,' he says. It just happened.

'I guess.'

He has a face out of Norway or somewhere that never looks me in the eye. Other than that, he's just a friend of my brother.

'Are you bored?' he says.

'No.' I must seem off, but I feel like myself.

'You sure?' he says.

When I don't answer, he writes in a notebook. That's him. He's always scribbling there. No one can read what he's written. It locks, just in case.

'Let's do it.'

He shuts the notebook, and fits it into his backpack. 'I can't remember what I did before I knew you and Jim,' he says. Jim's my brother.

'Not much.'

A senior is paying me five hundred dollars to kill him. Actually,

Pete got the job. But he asked me to help. I don't know the senior's name or what his problem is yet. I like the boy just enough to pretend like we're friends. He's not my thing, but he's an awful example of someone's, I guess. Two days ago, as a favor to me, Jude got drunk enough to seduce him. I pretended to pass out, then watched. It upset me so much that I decided to kill him already. So I guess it worked. She and I haven't talked about any of that, but it changed me. There are little behavioral things, I can tell. Like this afternoon. Before I took off, I told her she didn't love me enough. Then she said almost the same thing more angrily to me. After I left, I got upset about that. Maybe after I've killed him, I'll shoot myself in the head. That's different.

We're driving to Jude's parents' cabin. It's east of town in this resort where some friends of hers snowboard. She drew me a crude map. We're still in the desert somewhere, but I can see something big that's a mountainous shape. It's very black outside the car, except for this twinkling to the left. To me it looks like a town, but, according to him, it's too sparse. Otherwise, we haven't said anything in a while.

'I know,' he says.

'Know what?' I don't see how he could.

'I'll tell you later.'

We decide to eat something. I want to sit down, and there's an uncrowded IHOP. It's just like the millions all over the country. He orders pancakes, and pulls out his notebook. I order a steak, because it takes longer to cook. Then I pretend to take a leak, and find the pay phone.

'Pete, it's me.' He's already there at the cabin with Jude, but I know she won't fuck him. She likes tall, introverted, thin guys like myself.

'Yeah,' he says. ' Wait a second. Ssh.'

'We're on our way.'

'Where are you?' he says. 'Shut up, Jude. I can't hear.'

A year ago, I accidentally killed my friend Rand. He'd gotten in deep shit with drugs, and had to sell me his car. But he flipped out on me about that, and I punched him too hard. No one blamed me, so I didn't. That's not totally true, but when Pete asked me to help him out on this thing, I was fine. The boy thinks it's interesting about Rand. For a while, he asked me if I liked hitting people. When I finally said no, he cried. He's deep, which is why I've procrastinated. That's my thing, human depth. But when I saw him fuck Jude, I realized the depths to which I'd have to go.

'How was your food?' I say, sitting. My steak's here.

'Good.' He's slumped down, and hardly ate or wrote.

'What's up with you?'

'I'll tell you later,' he says. Then he watches me eat with that serious look he's been giving a lot. I swear it's trust. It looks like nothing else.

We've pulled off the highway, and onto a dirt road. We're sitting side by side on the hood. It's so warm. When you imagine the stars are a far away, upside-down city at night they seem more important. I learned that trick from him, but he's better at it.

'I know,' he says, after a lot of silence.

'Know what?'

'What's happening,' he says.

I'm not sure if he means about being killed, or if he means in the sky, or what. 'Yeah?'

'That night with Jude,' he says.

'So she told you.' That seems ambiguous enough.

'I saw it in your eyes,' he says.

'Bullshit.'

'And now too,' he says. He slides off the hood, then I hear the car's passenger door creak.

'See what?'

'But first, will you do me a favor?' he says. Then he hands me his unlocked notebook and a flashlight.

His notebook is so intense in some parts, I almost cried, and started skipping around. Words were my thing until Rand died, and I figured out they're too simple. Now I only read books about death. Maybe it's like how the boy gets off more on a pattern of lights than on what's really lit up. I mean that I like to think books about death are secretly about life. Maybe I can't explain it.

'Do you hate me now?' he says. We're driving again, and I'm thinking.

'You're a good writer.'

'Thanks,' he says. 'So we're going to see Jude?' I just told him we were.

'I figured you'd like that.'

I guess he needs to think for a second. 'It's fair,' he says.

This is hard. 'You want to wait until tomorrow?'

'Yeah,' he says.

'Because . . .' I can't finish. The why's too intense. It has partly to do with what I read in his notebook.

He waits for a second, I guess in case I do. 'Yeah, I know,' he says. I think he actually might. So it's just more intense.

From what I read, the boy's mom was a whore until somebody killed her. She never bothered to name him. I knew that. He was always the boy. When he was ten, she started selling his ass as a sideline. I didn't know that. When his ass earned more money than hers, she got jealous and beat him. Some men freaked out, and beat the shit out of him. At some point, he freaked out, and started burning and cutting himself with a knife. I didn't know that. Then the damage he did got so bad, the men wouldn't pay, and she dropped him off at his grandma's. Then she got killed. His grandma named him Bill, but it's not legal.

'Jude. Tell Pete I'm going to be late.'

'Where are you?' she says. 'It's Larry, Pete.'

'I don't know.'

'Oh, fuck,' she says. That means something. I know her.

'What?'

There's a pause on her end, and Pete's voice saying something I can't understand in the background.

'No, what?'

'I'll just feel better when you're here,' she says.

'Me, too.' Maybe I'll kill Pete.

He just took a shower. I'm sitting on the bed. When he fucked Jude, neither one of them took off their clothes, so I'm sort of in shock.

'Almost ready,' he says. He starts looking through his backpack for something clean to wear.

'Yeah.' I don't know what else to say.

His arms are all crisscrossed with cuts, scrapes, and little notches. His chest, back, and stomach are equally scarred all to hell in different ways, and his legs are slightly zigzagged from having been broken and not repaired right, if at all. Worst, his dick's really small, like he never grew up, and I guess it's been burned, or else partly cut off.

'How's she doing?' he says.

'Fine. I don't know.'

'You know I'm not in love with her,' he says.

'I know. Hurry up.'

'You know I'm not in love with Jim, either,' he says.

'I know, but let's not talk about that.'

We drive back to this truckstop I noticed. I'd figured the girls hanging out there were whores. A few of them are, but they're not all that young. They're seated around a picnic table drinking beer with some truckers. I let him choose our whore, and she gets in the car. It costs me extra to watch, but that's the point. When we reach the motel, she goes right in the bathroom. He gets undressed, and lies down on the bed. I start to strip, then change my mind when he looks at my chest. I'm too thin, and Jude tells me my hips stick too far out like a girl's. So I pull the shirt back on.

The whore's a lot heavier set than she looked, with this huge, pocked ass. 'Oh, my God,' she says, seeing his body.

'Sit on his face.' It's the meanest thing I can imagine.

She straddles his face, and starts to masturbate him. Once in a while, she lifts her ass, and lets him take a breath.

'Don't do that. If he can't breathe, that's not your problem.'

'What in the world?' she says.

His hand leaves her thigh, and searches around on the bedding, maybe for me. But I'm not even close.

'I'll pay you whatever you want. And no one will know.'

His hand's moving around. I can't decide if I should sit over there, and let him find me, or stand here, and if wanting to sit over there means I'm gay.

'He's a child,' she says.

'It's okay. He wants to suffer.'

About then his hand gives up on me, and makes a fist. It hits the bed.

'Sick fuck,' she says, and sits down hard on his face, then nervously crosses her arms.

'All your weight.'

The boy's sick to his stomach in the bathroom. Since he's on his knees over the toilet, that's loud. She saved his life, at the last second. I could have made her keep going. It's his notebook. I wish I'd never read it, or else waited. The whore just yelled something in Spanish, and left. I feel like that stuff with her wasn't enough or seemed too short. By the time I got my pants off, it was over.

'What are you thinking?' says his voice.

'I don't know.'

'You're nervous,' says his voice.

'Maybe.'

'I'm nervous too,' says his voice.

'Yeah, you don't understand.'

I don't know what's going on, but I walk in the bathroom. He doesn't get up or even turn. That gets me upset, so I take off my t-shirt and pull it over his face. Then I punch him so hard in the back, he falls forward, and hits his forehead. Blood is staining my shirt, so I pull it off, and force him to face me. He doesn't look like he understands what I'm doing at all, which is confusing. I've just grabbed his throat, so he'll realize how violent I'm ready to get.

'You understand?'

'Yeah,' he says. He won't look at me.

'Don't do that.'

'Do what?' he says.

'I swear to God.'

I throw the punch that killed Rand. It clips his nose, and gives him a flash walrus moustache of blood. He grabs his nose, and says not to hit him again, but I do. He tries to crawl away, so the blow clips the back of his head, and seems to knock him unconscious. But he could be pretending. I wouldn't put it past him.

'Pete. Jesus fucking Christ.' I just told Jude that I was really upset, and to put his stupid ass on the phone.

'You sound strange,' he says.

'Why does the guy want him dead?'

'I thought you didn't want to know the . . .' he says.

'Just tell me.'

'Don't . . .' he says.

'Just fucking tell me.'

The senior's an acquaintance of ours, Gilman Crowe. It's about the boy's notebook, Pete says. That wasn't the reason until I told Pete, and I guess he told Gilman. Knowing Pete, he thinks it's something gay. I think it probably has to do with how Gilman's the head of this Nazi style group. But I don't care enough, and Pete won't say. He's just supposed to kill the boy, bring Gilman the notebook, and get paid.

'Okay, no problem.'

'I know it's fucked up,' Pete says. He means how he just asked me to wait so he can watch, and how I owe him.

'Everything is.'

'Whatever,' Pete says. That reminds me.

'If you fuck Jude, I'll kill you.'

The boy just woke up, or quit faking. I was on my knees, wondering if I should stop what I was doing to him, or maybe kill Pete instead, but I couldn't decide. Anyway, I was crying with my face in his hair when he came back around, so I ran out here and sat down on the bed. I can see him in the mirror.

'It's okay,' he says. His voice is raspy and choked, either from when I was strangling him, or he could be sad, too.

'You keep saying that.'

'It's okay,' he says, and looks at me. His reflection does, I mean. 'I like you.'

'No, it's not.'

'That's why I let you read my notebook,' he says.

For some reason, I suddenly figure out what he's been saying he knows. Or else I let myself think it. Then it takes me a second or two to make sure. This is really hard. 'Jim told you?'

The boy turns, I mean all the way around and looks right at me for real. It's intense. 'Yeah,' he says.

'What did he say?' Then I start crying again. It's the end.

I guess he thinks I want to talk, but I can't even move. Anyway, he comes out of the bathroom, and stands in front of me. When I don't do anything, he puts his arms around my neck.

'Oh, God.' I put my arms around his waist.

'What?' he says.

'Nothing.' It could have been so different.

Rand died from a punch to the face. Afterwards, he seemed fine, just a little dizzy. There wasn't even blood. I guess he died in his sleep. That part about me hitting him is the truth. But it wasn't the car or the drugs. It's because he got all protective of Jim. I knew he liked my brother, but I thought it was nothing. Anyway, that turned out to be bullshit. I got to keep his car when he died. When Jude and I cleaned it out this one time, we found some naked pictures he'd taken of Jim. They're hidden in my bedroom. She doesn't know I didn't throw them away, or tell Jim, or what that means. When Rand died, I turned into this.

If it wasn't for words, I wouldn't know how to put lies between me and everyone else, just by how I use them. I used to talk a lot, but now it's sparse. Jude says you can feel me in there, but it doesn't add up to that much, even when you know me. I guess she's the only one who still wonders why not.

The cabin's at the end of a long, unmarked dirt road. I couldn't find it at first. I hug Jude, but she pushes me off. I think she's just pissed that the boy is with me. I guess Pete didn't tell her. The boy seems confused about Pete being there, so he sits on a couch, and starts to write in his notebook. I can't tell what he's thinking. He writes for a while, then shuts the notebook, and puts it away in his backpack. By now, Pete's saying sarcastic things about the boy being gay, and just told him to strip.

'Pete, come on.'

'I'm sorry,' the boy says. He's bunched himself into a ball on the couch, and Pete's laughing and trying to undress him.

'Jude, say something.'

'Don't, please,' the boy says.

Pete gets him straightened out on his stomach, and pulls down his underwear and jeans. 'Someone's had some fun,' he says.

'Fuck you. Jude?' She's somewhere around, and I need her to hug me right now. So I feel the air behind me.

'Jesus Christ,' Pete says. He just ripped the boy's shirt off, and saw all the scars.

'What,' she says. That sounded angry.

'Tell Pete to stop.'

'Why?' she says. So I guess they did fuck.

Jude just read the boy's notebook, or the part about sleeping with her. I held the book, so she couldn't read anything about me. She's crying, and I almost am too. We're over by the couch, talking softly to him. Pete just kicked the boy in the stomach and back. Then I finally told Jude about the murder for hire. Pete's in the other room, reading the notebook. I insisted. I fucking threw it at him. I don't care if he reads all the parts about me, and I kind of hope he will.

'Look, we'll stop this,' Jude says, and strokes the boy's hair.

'Seriously?' he says.

'Yeah,' she says. 'Somehow.'

'I don't know,' he says. He looks down at his legs, and I think tries to move them around. But they don't stir, and he gets this shocked look on his face.

'We will.'

'Shut the fuck up, Larry,' she says.

'I want to die,' the boy says.

'No, you don't. I read your notebook. I know you don't.'

I hear a fluttery noise, then what sounds like the boy's notebook hitting a wall. Pete walks back into the room, looking incredibly annoyed. 'Yeah, so?' he says.

'Did you read it?'

'I read it,' Pete says. 'He wishes he was dead. Big news.'

'No, he doesn't,' Jude says.

'Sure he does,' Pete says.

'No, he doesn't.'

I look at the boy, but he's looking at Pete. There's something about what's going on in his eyes. Or that he's showing it to Pete. I don't know why, but that does it. It makes me start to cry and punch him really hard in the face.

'Whoa,' Pete says, and laughs.

'No, you fucking don't.'

Jude and I are in the basement. I was walking around dazedly in the woods when she found me. No one's supposed to go down

here at all. If you do, you have to carry a flashlight. The floor's
dirt. Pete tried to bury him here, but the ground was too hard. I
told Pete if he wants any money, the body's his job. So he carried
the boy back upstairs, and burned him in the fireplace. We're
repairing Pete's damage. He was kneeling in front of the fireplace
the last time I checked, jabbing the smoke with a poker.

'You're both monsters,' Jude says. She means it isn't just Pete.
I've been ragging about him. I don't know what else to do.

'Why don't you shut up?'

'You are,' she says. She is, too, and I'm almost positive
they fucked.

'I'll buy you a car.' For some reason that's important.

'Fuck you,' she says.

'It's true. It's so totally true, and I think that's so totally
important.'

'What are you talking about?' she says.

We're outside by Jude's car, and she won't look at me. I'm so sick
of people doing that. Pete is sitting shotgun in mine, and just
honked the horn. So I guess I have to say it. 'I love you, Jude.'

'How can you say that?' she says, sounding really tired. She
pulls the car keys from her pocket.

'Look, I'm sorry. It's just that ever since Rand, I don't care.'

She gets in the car, and shuts the door. It happens so fast that
she must be reacting to what I just said. She puts the key in the
ignition, and acts like she's going to leave. Then she rolls down
the window. 'So, did you ask him about Jim?' she says.

'No.' I did, but I have to tell her I didn't. I can't explain why.
It's between her and me.

'And you killed him anyway,' she says. Then she seems to get
upset, and starts the car. 'I can't believe it.'

'Yeah, so what?'

*   *   *

The notebook's in my trunk, but Pete agreed to say it got burned. Either that, or I'll tell everyone that Pete's gay. So he's pissed off, and saying how I'm the one who's gay and insane and a liar. Then we get to Gilman's house. His bedroom's painted black, and has some chairs for his Nazi group meetings. I went to one, but couldn't make up my mind. There's a poster of Harris and Kliebald, the two Columbine guys. Gilman made it in Photoshop, and put the words 'Coming Soon' across the top so his parents would think they're a rock band. They're his heroes, and that's part of my problem. Of all the guys who shot other guys at their high schools back then, they're so boring.

'So, yeah,' Gilman says. He didn't expect me to be here with Pete. I don't know what would have happened if I wasn't. 'I guess we'll talk.'

'Yeah.' He just offered me money to kill Pete, and even gave me a gun. It's in my pocket. Pete was in the bathroom, but he came back before Gilman told me why everyone has to die.

'Let's go,' Pete says.

'So, did you read the notebook?' Gilman says.

'No, I don't care.'

'I read it,' Pete says. 'But I already knew you were gay.' Then he punches Gilman's shoulder, I guess to make it seem more of a joke.

'Right,' Gilman says. He looks at me.

'Let's go,' Pete says.

'Okay?' Gilman says to me, meaning the thing about Pete, I guess. I don't know what else it would mean. 'We're cool?'

I look at Pete. 'Yeah, we're cool.'

I need something to drink, so we're paused in this Mexican

drive-through. It's not one of the big, famous places. Jude worked here last summer, which is how I know about it. If you tip the guy at the window, he adds a bag of grass to your order. It's a gift for Jude. I'm trying to decide when and where to kill Pete, or if I should, and a good excuse to go somewhere, and what I feel about Pete. First, I need to know for sure.

'So, did you fuck her?'

'You're joking,' Pete says, and laughs.

'So you didn't.'

I guess he thinks about that while I drive to the window, and get the bags. 'So that boy liked you a lot, I guess,' he says.

'Yeah, I guess.' I pull out my Pepsi, and wedge the cup into my crotch. But it's cold and too close to my balls, so I have to adjust it.

'You know Kliebald was gay,' he says. He glances at my crotch, which is sort of why I did that little thing with the cup, as a test. I mean thinking he might.

'No, he wasn't.'

'Sure he was,' Pete says. 'He told people. He was in love with Harris, but Harris wasn't gay. So they did that Columbine thing instead of having sex. That's why they did it.'

'Okay, whatever.'

'Look it up on the fucking web,' he says.

'Fine, whatever. Jesus.' Then I remember that spot in the hills where you can see the town's lights, and no one goes except for gay guys and people like me and the boy. 'I'm not gay, okay? I don't want you to get the wrong idea.'

'Larry, come on,' he says, and laughs.

'Anyway, there's this fire road at the top of Myrtle Street, and you can walk up, and there are all these trees. It's nice.'

'I heard about it,' he says.

'So you want to go?'

'Like on a date?' he says. That's sarcastic. People I know use sarcasm to hide around me. They've figured out that if they don't act completely sincere, I won't understand, and will get upset.

'Just say what you want to say, Pete.' Then I slam my fist down on the steering wheel.

I'm on a pay phone near Jude's, and Pete is still in my car. We got to where the fire road begins, but I couldn't get out.

'Jude, pick up if you're there.' There's the click.

'I was so mad at you,' she says. I know her, and picking up is a sign of her loving me again, and how she can't help herself. 'So did you get the money?'

'Yeah, I'm with Pete. Can we come over? I need to know something.'

She doesn't say anything. 'God, you're so fucked up,' she says.

'Gilman wants me to kill him. I don't know what to do.'

'I'm tired,' she says.

'I know you guys fucked, okay?'

She's freaking out in secret. I can't describe how I know that. 'Okay, come over,' she says. 'But you need help.'

Pete and Jude are sitting on her futon. He took everything off but his socks and underwear, but she won't strip. There used to be pictures of me on her bulletin board, but she's taken them down since I was here yesterday. So I guess I'm even quieter than usual, and tired.

'Go ahead.' I'm standing with my arms crossed.

'Look, Larry,' Pete says. They're really stoned, and want to talk. Maybe I should just shoot them both. 'I like you. You're an interesting guy. But I know you're in love with me or something, and it's cool, but I'm just not.'

'I'm sorry,' Jude says.

I wasn't expecting any of that, and it confuses me. She looks scared, and he looks arrogant, so I don't know what to say to them now. 'Bullshit.'

'She told me not to tell you,' he says.

'It's okay,' she says to him.

'Anyway, she said you're probably bisexual,' he says.

'Yeah, well, I'm straight.'

Pete looks anxiously at Jude, who isn't looking at either one of us now. 'Well, she said you watched her do it with other guys,' he says.

'I don't know. Maybe I'm confused.'

'That's what I think she meant,' he says.

'He knows about you and Jim,' Jude says to me.

'It's cool,' Pete says.

'I'm sorry, Larry,' she says. 'It just slipped out.'

'It's cool,' Pete says to her. 'Seriously, if I was drunk enough, I'd do his brother.'

'God, Jude.'

'I'm sorry,' she says to Pete.

Then I can't talk, and lose it, and start to cry, but she doesn't come over and hug me. Pete doesn't either, or even make one of his stupid ass jokes. So I pull out the gun and point it where it belongs. I just want them to know.

Rand died when I punched him too hard in the face. But it wasn't my fault. I just ended a life that was going to end any second. He had a thing in his brain that nobody realized was there. He was born with it. That's why I'm not in jail, and why no one blames me, not even his parents. He did something to Jim, so I hit him. That part's true. But what he did was tell Jim that what we'd been doing together was sick, because he accidentally found out. I didn't know how Rand secretly felt about me, or I did but wouldn't let myself know. Then Jude and I found those naked pictures Rand took, and I got so upset that I told her about me and Jim. I still don't know why Rand took them, or why Jim didn't tell me. I still don't know what either one of them secretly felt about me or each other. That's what ultimately killed me, I think.

My dad always sits in the same chair. It's in the livingroom, so you can't get around him. I just forget he's sick until I get him pissed off, and he tries to stand up. My mom's standing by the chair, in case I get him upset, and he tries that again.

'I swear to God.' I'm telling him why I was out all last night, and didn't call. I know it sounds like everything else. He can't think, or maybe can't tell anyone what he thinks, if he does. 'You can call her parents.'

'Look,' he says, and tries to think. I remember how that looked. It's pointless now, though. It just makes him look scared. 'Okay.'

'Tom,' my mom says. That's his name. She can't change his mind anymore, because it's nowhere to begin with. He's got cancer.

'I won't do it again.'

'No, you won't,' he says. That's pretty good for him.

'Then I'm going upstairs.' First I wait for him or her to suggest something else. It's embarrassing, but I really wish they would. I don't know what we could do, maybe go out to eat or see a movie.

They just wait for me to leave. Dad already found my shotgun, and some grass that Jude left here one time. Then Mom blocked off half of the internet. So I guess they think the upstairs is as safe as it's going to get.

*   *   *

I'm halfway there, and wondering if Jim's around, when my mom comes up behind me with the notebook.

'Honey,' she says. I've gotten to like how that sounds, even if it's a deeper word than I can deal with right now. It's just so soft.

'Yeah.'

'You forgot this,' she says, and hands it over.

'Oh, right.'

'There's a lot going on around here,' she says, I guess as an apology for not being angrier at me. When my dad got sick, we just fell apart. All four of us.

'I'm cool.'

'Meaning you'll be okay,' she says, and smiles in this sarcastic way that looks terrifying on her. I don't remember when that started. Little things like that, I don't know.

'Yeah, sure.'

I'm at my desk, searching what's left of the web for anything about ghosts, and don't care again. Maybe crying helped. Jude's on the phone. She left a bunch of freaked out messages, but now she sounds stoned.

'You scared me,' she says. Then I hear Pete's voice. 'Oh, Pete says it's cool, and . . . it never happened, and . . . what, Pete? Yeah, just that.'

'Did you tell him about the Gilman thing?'

'No,' she says. 'But I say . . . don't do it.'

'Of course you do.'

'What?' she says, I guess to Pete, because I hear him in there. Then she laughs. 'I'm not going to tell him. You tell him.'

'Tell me what?'

'Pete just made a stupid joke,' she says, sounding nervous. Then

I guess the phone either gets swiped from her or Pete puts his mouth closer to hers.

'Hey,' he says, sounding maybe drunk now on top of being stoned. Whenever I think about him, he's always drunk. But when he's actually drunk, I never know what to say to him. 'Larry?'

'Yeah.'

'Jude says I should tell you,' he says. Then I hear her tell him not to say it. 'It's not a joke, Jude.' But he laughs.

'He's drunk, Larry,' she yells to me from wherever.

'Say it, Pete.'

I check my email. There's just a bunch of junk mail from paranormal themed sites, except for one. It's from the Franks, who can supposedly hear the dead talk. I saw them on TV, then wrote to them at the address on their website. They travel around, and you hire them. They walk through haunted houses and graveyards with a special tape recorder, asking questions. Then they put what they recorded through software that brings out details in what just sounds like the wind. Sometimes they find voices that answer their questions, or say related things only dead, confused people would think. I guess I want to hear Rand one more time before I stop worrying about him. Anyway, the Franks are coming out here on their tour, and say they'll call. That's great, but it doesn't change the fact.

'Larry,' Pete says. I just answered the phone. He sounds more drunk. Plus I can hear the sounds of a store, maybe the small liquor store that's walking distance from here.

'Yeah.' This could be it. He said he'd call and finally tell me whatever.

'You aren't mad?' he says.

'I don't know. Just tell me.'

'I don't know, either,' he says. 'Look, I didn't fuck her.'

'It's okay.' Maybe he's crying, not drunk.

'Shit,' he says. 'Look, I . . .' Then I hear a bunch of cars go by, and some things vaguely happening in the store. 'I have to tell you something, but I can't.'

'Gilman paid me to kill you.'

I guess he's crying. 'I said I'd tell you,' he says, sounding angry. 'You don't have to . . . Fuck, Larry. Forget it.'

'Pete?'

Jim's in his bedroom, listening to music. It has to have an acoustic guitar or piano and vocals, but not too much else. That's his thing. If you're in the bathroom, like I am, you can hear some of the lyrics through the strangely thin wall. He never says much to me anymore, so I think they're important. It's a song about love. That's why I'm here, and so nervous.

'Jim.' That used to be our signal.

I hear him turn down the music. He used to leave it up, and there would be a minute while he was taking off his clothes. Then he'd say my name back, and I'd go in there, and lock the door behind me. That's what I remember.

'I'm sorry.'

The music's still down, which means something.

'What do you want?' he says.

I didn't expect that. He knows. It hasn't been all that long, but it scares me that he'd ask. 'I don't know.'

I wait, and he probably waits. I've never said I didn't know what I want, and he's never turned down the music, so I guess we're confused. He's only thirteen, and I'm supposed to be aggressive.

'Okay, I do.'

I know he's lying on his bed. He'd have to be there, or I couldn't hear him. He moved his bed to the other side of this wall about two years ago, and he hasn't moved it back. I check all the time.

There's this little metal sound that barely gets through the wall. It's almost nothing, but it lets me see inside myself like if it was a star or a word. It's the snap on his jeans.

'Jim.'

The wall thuds, because he hit it. I know him. Then it thuds a bunch of times. So I guess he's upset, but I know he's undressed. He doesn't have to say my name.

2

I'm at breakfast. It's always something easy to make like a cold cereal. Dad watches taped golf from the weekend, and my mom reads the paper. Something in her is going off about me. I can see it's not the world. Jim's food is already a ruin, which is the only thing wrong.

'Jim rode his bike,' she says. Not hello, or anything. That's news, since I always drive him to school.

'Yeah?'

She turns a page fast, and it rips. But I'm tired enough from one or maybe two hour's sleep, that her shit doesn't reach me.

'Say it, mom.'

'Your dad had a cramp, and I was up, and I saw you,' she says.

'Meaning what?' I'm pretty sure I was naked, and holding my clothes and my shoes in a wad.

'I called Dr. Thorne,' she says.

'What did Jim say?'

'He protected you,' she says.

'From what?' I throw my cereal bowl at the wall.

I think Rand is still on the floor of my bedroom. I mean in

some way. I know he didn't die there. He got up after a couple of minutes, and left. But I think he'd come there if he could go anywhere. That's the Franks' big idea, or their excuse. The dead don't want to be dead, and they only give a shit about life. When I got back to my bedroom last night, I thought a lot about Rand, then decided. I killed the boy because I can't kill myself. That's why I hit him so hard. I realize he isn't Jim. When I get that upset, it doesn't take much to remind me.

I always hang out with Will. Sometimes Tran is there too. They're what's left of my friends. Everyone else thinks I'm cold. Will and Tran are so into themselves, they don't notice. We like to watch the other students show up, and talk angrily about them. It's mostly Will. They're still too sleepy to hate us. When they do, I'll definitely feel it. It usually takes until lunch.

'I didn't sleep.' Will's noticed something in me, but that'll probably do it. He used to go out with Jude, which is our mutual thing.

'Her again?' he says.

'Yeah.'

'So surprising,' Tran says. He's a mistake I almost made five or six times when I used to get drunk. As friends, we're all figured out and boring.

'Did you hear about the freak?' Will says. He means the boy, and I'm the one who started calling him that. He was just Jim's weirdest friend at the time.

'What about him?'

'He's been going to Gilman's meetings,' Will says.

I look at Tran. So if I react to the news, they'll misinterpret. I told Will I hate Tran, and Tran thinks he knows me. It's complicated. 'That's weird.'

'Seriously, what's up with you?' Will says.

'What does it seem like?'

Tran gives me this look. It would be hard to describe. He tries it out on me every few days. If I give it back, we're both probably dead.

I gave Tran the look, but I was going for spaced. I can't be sure it wasn't in there somewhere. His dad's white, and there's not that much bug in his face. That might just be it. He used to mix me up when I was drunk and confused about whether I missed Jim or not. But nothing ever happened. We're walking to Algebra class, and every glance I give him is a warning. That's how I see it.

'What time?' Tran says. It means should he come by my house. He sounds cold but isn't, which is our usual mutual thing.

I just shrug. It doesn't matter when.

'It's been a while,' he says. He means since I've wanted to be around him without Will. That's how backwardly he understands me.

'Too long.'

'You're so strange,' he says. I just felt him bump against me. That's pushing it. We're in fucking public. He's not there yet, if ever. It'll take concentration or beer.

'Don't be stupid.'

After Rand died, I was drunk for a month, even at school. People I didn't already know thought it was tragic, and left me alone. The things with Tran and Pete started then. It had been building, and I'd just let anything happen. Tran was a bug who kept looking at me, and Pete was a popular guy who'd turned into a drunk for some reason. I thought drunkenness would be my life. I thought not questioning things before I said them was telling the truth. I thought if someone was nice to me when I was drunk, he was gay. I thought if I liked someone when I was drunk, I was gay. When I was drunk, I'd do anything not to have hit Rand.

School tends to go one of two ways in the mornings. People's hatred for me is still vague and wearing off, unless I push it. That's one way. Or it's just about the teachers and me, and preparing for what's going to happen at lunch, and maybe something with Jude after school. Today I just want to find Pete, and avoid Gilman Crowe in the halls. That's my major worry, but he's nowhere around. No one brings up the boy's empty desks in the classes we shared. He's just some black shit in the ground, and that was happening with or without me. Or that's what I've decided his notebook is actually about.

I put my arm around Jude. Most students eat lunch in groups of two up to eight on the grass. It's like a park. Otherwise, you eat on benches around the park's edge facing them like an audience. That's just safer.

'You allright?'

'Jesus, Larry,' she says. 'No, for a million reasons.'

'Check this out . . .'

'I can't take it,' she says, and shrugs until I've taken my arm off her shoulders.

'I'm not gay.'

'What?' she says, and laughs. She's started to look to her left and my right.

'I know it now. And you want to know why?'

'You're so fucked up,' she says. 'It scares me.'

Gilman's talking to Pete, who looks drunk. It's the wobble. When he gets drunk enough, he'll say or do anything. That's the rumor. They're standing next to the wall where the school's insignia is painted. It's gigantic and very bleached out. It is or was a bulldog.

'It's just Jim. That's all.'

'What?' Jude says. She was busy with Pete. 'What are you talking about?'

'Jim's the one who's gay.'

'Yeah,' she says sarcastically. 'That's got to be it.'

I hear Pete yell. By the time I look over, Gilman's already gone, and Pete is looking at us or just Jude. I guess no one noticed me here until they followed his eyes. Now I can feel their mean, snickering bullshit.

'Can I come by later?' I've gotten to my feet. They'll stop turning into assholes as soon as I'm gone, or I won't know it at least. I mean it's not about Jude.

'Yeah,' she says. 'I guess we should talk.'

Pete's walking away down this hall. It doesn't go anywhere, and dead ends just behind the girls' gym. It's where the school stores things it only needs once a year, like the stage for graduation. It used to be where you'd smoke cigarettes. Since Columbine, it's watched over by cameras, so it's where students go when they need the school's help.

'Pete.' That was a loud whisper.

He looks back at me for a second, then keeps walking, and raises one hand to mean stop or I'm okay. 'I'll tell you tonight,' he says.

'We need to talk.'

He gets to a cinderblock wall, and leans against it. Then he turns his head, and sees me watching him, I guess. 'Fuck. I'll tell you.'

'What was up with Gilman?'

'Nothing,' he says. 'The guy's an asshole.'

'Why were you crying last night?'

'Why are you doing this?' Pete says. I think he's crying again. 'I'm just trying to think for five fucking minutes. I haven't been thinking all fucking day.'

'Because I'm confused.'

'Can't you wait?' he says. His voice is a rag.

Gilman is standing with two of his shaved headed, t-shirt and jeans wearing crowd. I just left Pete, and turned a corner. I know one of them, Jeanne, who's his girlfriend. I think they were waiting for Pete, and seem surprised.

'What's Pete doing?' Gilman says. His hands are punched in the pockets of his jeans. So I punch my hands in mine. You have to do that with him.

'Hey,' Jeanne says. She used to be my girlfriend. I make her act tense because I know why she turned into a Nazi. It's not supposed to be personal.

'Chilling, I think. Hey, Jeanne.'

'Are we cool?' Gilman says. He's really studying me. It's weirdly nice.

'I'm seeing Pete tonight.'

'He said,' Gilman says. 'Where?'

I have to think about that for a second. 'The hill.' Then I watch him.

He has a boney and glaring white face that talks politics all the time, so getting deep enough into his eyes is a puzzle. 'Come by after,' he says.

'Look, I don't know if I can kill Pete.'

'What?' Gilman says. He looks at Rick and Jeanne, who make these faces like they didn't know about that. Then he stares angrily at the ground.

'But I have this other idea.'

'I don't care,' Gilman says.

It's my last class today, and the one where I used to do well. It's journalism, but I'm beyond it. You write articles about the school for the high school newspaper. We're supposed to be thinking up new ones. I was in my head, with a gun aimed at Pete. We were in the woods. I couldn't decide if he was naked or what else had already happened. So when I see the world again, I'm confused.

'Larry,' the teacher says. I think that was the second time he did.

'Yeah?'

This Black soccer coach just walked into the classroom. He said something secretive to the teacher, and sat on the edge of the desk. Then they shot me the same, confusing look. I'm never the point of anything in this class, so most students did too.

'You're friends with Pete Hampton?' the teacher says.

'Sort of.'

'They're friends,' the coach says quietly, and rubs one of his giant, bare legs.

Someone laughs, because I almost never talk. It might be the 'sort of' thing too, since Pete's such an alchoholic. Or it could be how gay the coach seems when you're dressed.

'Larry,' the teacher says again. The coach is back on his feet, and almost everyone's laughing around me. So it takes me a second.

'Oh, right.'

Pete was a star on the soccer team last year. I wrote an article about it. But he lost interest last summer, and quit. I wasn't there. People who liked him back then blame the people who like him right now. I'm one of maybe three. The Black coach

seems to like Pete both ways, but that's a secret. The rumor is
Pete got too drunk and let the coach fool around. I started that.
We share a gym class, and Pete's locker's near mine. The coach
is always hanging around to make sure no one fights. But he just
watches Pete get undressed, like I do. Sometimes we catch each
other looking, and stop. It's so obvious.

We're in an office that's set aside for the coaches. There's no
bookshelf, just soccer posters from Europe. I've only seen it from
the hall. Pete's slumped down in a chair, and I'm standing with
my arms tightly crossed.

'You cool?'

'Yeah, I'm fucking great,' Pete says.

'So what's Pete's problem?' the coach says to me. He's sitting
between us on top of his desk, but that doesn't seem as gay here.
'In your mind.'

'Fuck you,' Pete says to him.

'I don't know.' I said that like I didn't, then smiled like I
secretly did.

'No idea?' he says.

'I think Pete's gay and doesn't want to be.'

'That's such bullshit,' Pete says, and looks out the window.

'Why do you think that?' the coach says to me.

'We're both going out with the same girl. That's what she
thinks.'

'More bullshit,' Pete says.

'I think the problem is his friends,' the coach says.

'Larry's not my friend,' Pete says.

'So what are you?' the coach says to me. Then we both look
at Pete, and wait.

'Two guys who are fucking the same girl,' Pete says after a

second, and laughs sarcastically at us or maybe something out the window.

'All right,' the coach says, laughing too. He slaps Pete's shoulder. Then they both look confusingly at me.

Pete's shotgun in my car with a cup of sloshing coffee. The nurse made it for him, after school suspended him for a week. The coach let me leave early so I could give him a ride.

'Please, Larry,' he says. He doesn't want to go home, and just asked me again to hang out until later. I can't tell if I'm still upset about that crack about Jude, or just pretending I am.

'I have a doctor's appointment.'

'What's the difference?' he says. He means if he waits in the car. That's already established, but I forgot. I'm nervous.

'So you're still going to tell me.'

Pete slides down low in the seat, and puts his shoes up on the dashboard. It's a different decision, I guess. I'm not gay. Then he looks at the coffee cup, and turns it around and around. It's red, but doesn't have a pattern. So that's nerves, too.

'So are you?'

'Yeah,' he says. 'If you promise . . .'

'Obviously.'

He thinks about that, or something else, and keeps revolving his cup. The traffic light's red, so we're stopped. Dr. Thorne's office is maybe eight blocks away. So I decide to do something to Pete because I can ask what it means about me in a minute.

'Shit,' Pete says afterwards. 'What the fuck?'

'I know, okay?'

I drove by Dr. Thorne's without thinking, and have to make an illegal U turn. I don't know what happened to the cup. It's not there, and he hasn't redone his jeans. I unzipped them. That's all I had time for. I guess he needs to think about what I did too. So I make the U, then park, and we sit here.

'I have to go.'

Pete's patting his leg. I know it could mean anything in the world. 'Then go,' he says.

There's a window facing out on the street. The walls are just very packed bookshelves. I try to concentrate on the spines while we talk. I mean the titles. They're my only way into his head, but they're just ways into mine. He doesn't realize I don't understand them. I'm especially cold around him, but he's the coldest.

'Why don't you talk about Jim?' he says.

I just made him get up and look out at my car, then admit Pete would be considered attractive, if you were gay or not. He's back in his chair, and I'm still in mine.

'He and I are cool.'

'Your problems with Jim began when your friend died,' he says.

'Well, you want me to say I wondered if I was gay.'

That takes him a second. 'And you're not wondering now?' he says.

'I'm not wondering at all.'

'Do you think you're in love with Jude?' he says.

'I don't know.'

'Do you think you're in love with Jim?' he says.

'Fuck you.'

'What would you say is the difference?' he says.

'That Jim's in love with me.'

He has to think about that. 'What did your mother see last night?' he says.

'She saw me walk down the hall.'

'You were naked,' he says.

'Yeah, and I guess she got off on it.' As soon as I say that,

I'm dead. I guess his books work, or one of them. It's also that I'm tired.

'What do you mean by that?' he says.

'That you're a fucking asshole.'

'Why am I a bleeping asshole?' he says.

'Because you know I don't want to talk about Jim.'

'What do you want to talk about?' he says.

'Do you think I'm gay?'

'Do you think you're gay?' he says.

'No. Do you think I'm gay?'

That takes him a second. 'I think the issue can't be resolved until you've had a consensual gay experience,' he says.

That takes me a second.. 'You're obsessed.'

'What am I obsessed with?' he says.

'With Jim.'

'How so?' he says.

'Because you don't even know Jim, but you keep talking about him.'

'Jim's in treatment with me,' he says.

That takes me a second. 'Why?'

'For depression,' he says.

'Okay.' Now I'm looking for something to throw. It would have to be a book. If I throw it at him, he'll ask why. He cares more about what I do wrong than my mom does.

'You're uncomfortable with that,' he says.

'No, I'm just surprised.'

'That's understandable,' he says.

'So what are you going to tell my mom?'

'That you've agreed to go back into treatment,' he says.

'Okay.' Then I get up and leave. It was time anyway. When your sessions are over, he picks up this pen so you'll know. He was looking at it.

*   *   *

Pete was asleep when I got back to the car. So I drove toward the hill, but I realized it's too light, and turned back. Then I parked by Jim's school, and moved the gun into my pocket. It was under the seat. Most kids have gone home, but Jim sometimes stays late to hang out with a teacher he likes. I just think if I see him, I'll decide. I know that's his red, scratched up bike.

'Where are we?' Pete says. I just unzipped his pants again to make sure, which I guess woke him up. He looks at Jim's school, and zips his pants.

'Here's an idea.'

'Jesus Christ,' he says. I don't think that's about anything. He's still getting a rush off the world.

'You know that guy Tran?'

'The ice skater bug,' he says. That's how people differentiate Tran. It's about his stiff posture, and what it makes out of the back of his pants. It's either gross or exciting, depending on if you're straight or maybe gay and drunk.

'What if we did it with him instead?'

He looks at me, and just blinks. 'Instead of what?' he says.

'Instead of what we were going to do.'

'Wow,' he says, and I guess tries to think a lot more, or more clearly. I watch him, then just happen to glance out the car.

'Duck down.'

Jim walks out of the school, sure enough with some teacher. It could be a man who has nothing to do with the school. They say something, or one of them does, and Jim unlocks his bike. When he's straddling it, and has ridden for part of a block, I start the car. Pete's sitting up by then, and we're driving.

'Do you think Jim's better looking than Tran?'

Pete looks at my eyes, then follows them to Jim's back. He got my mom's thin, blond, nervous thing. 'That's your brother?' he says, and squints. 'No, it's not.'

I speed up a little.

'Shit, what happened to him?' he says.

'He's depressed. And you're not drunk.'

Pete puts one hand up between Jim and his face, like Jim's the sun. He adjusts it a little, and shuts one eye. 'Oh, I get it,' he says.

'What?'

'You mean if I was shit faced drunk?' he says. 'And if Jude was there too?' If he says it, I'm going to kill him. That'll be the reason.

'Go for it.'

I hit Rand because of how he talked about Jim. It wasn't what he accused me of doing. Maybe I thought that was it. Later I realized it was the words he had used. They made Jim into someone who couldn't control what he felt, and made me into someone Rand didn't know better than anyone else. I didn't know you could change things with words, so it was intense. For a minute afterwards, I believed Rand. I guess he got me to admit to what Jim and I did. Then for a while after that, I saw Jim through Rand's eyes, and decided I was sick. So I thought if I hit Rand hard enough, it would stop.

I just introduced Pete to my mom. Dad's next. He's sitting out in the backyard. I can hear his radio. It's always tuned to some noisy talk station. That was the doctor's idea. Mom was gardening, from her clothes. I can tell she's had a couple of drinks, so I'm afraid of her face. It's not hers. That's what happens. It joins this insane women's club.

'So we're going upstairs, I guess.' We've established almost everything else, and it's now or not at all. 'Is Jim here?'

She's looking confusedly at Pete. He's handsome, so I guess she can't just see another one of my friends. 'You know Jim's friend Bill?' she says.

I can't see Pete's face, so I'm tense. 'Vaguely.'

'Not really,' Pete says.

'He's gone missing,' she says. Then something happens to her eyes, and she turns and looks at nothing. I think it's my dad.

'That's weird.'

'Jim's at Bill's grandmother's house,' she says. Then something in her makes the back of her head or hair shake. 'Your dad just told me he doesn't love me.'

'Hunh.'

I stole Pete two six packs of beer from the fridge. He's drinking the fourth, so he's not as nervous. He got belligerent about the thing with the boy, and decided to leave. He keeps saying he should, but he'll be too shit faced any minute. I know him. I thought it would take her much longer to figure things out. The grandmother, I mean. In his notebook, the boy disappears all the time.

'What's the matter?' Jim says. We're on the phone. His nose is usually stuffed up from some medication he takes, so I don't know if he's upset.

'Pete's here.' I said that like I wasn't okay.

'Oh, shit,' Pete says. He was looking through my old rack of CDs, but turned around at the sound of his name, then took another swallow.

'She's really upset,' Jim says. I guess I hear that in the background.

'But doesn't he always run away and stuff?'

'Tell him to bring a girl,' Pete says.

'What?' Jim says. Then I hear even deeper, less upset voices around him. 'I'm sorry. The police want me to get off the phone.'

'Come home, okay?'

Jim doesn't say anything for a second. He must know what I'm asking. 'One second,' he says. I think that was to the police. 'Why?'

'You know why.'

'So Larry can fuck you,' Pete says, and laughs. That was loud. So I guess he's shit faced enough. I guess it could have been sarcastic. Either way, he made me laugh, which I shouldn't have done without putting my hand on the phone.

'Pete's drunk.'

'What?' Jim says, I'm not sure to whom. It doesn't matter.

'Nothing.'

I just hit Pete, not that hard. It was either hit him, or turn gay. I think I was gay for a minute. He fell off the bed, and broke a videotape I don't own. Pete was tired of waiting for Jim, and I guess got impatient. I was afraid he would leave, so I started. I guess I didn't like it, or liked it too much. He's sitting on the floor. Rand was unconscious, so that's different.

'I can't believe this.' I mean what I was thinking before I hit Pete. I guess I'm crying, and have been crying for a minute.

'You're losing it,' Pete says. 'And you have to fucking not.'

'Maybe.' I just grabbed my knees, and pulled them close to my chest. That's never good. I know myself.

'Look, I don't care if you're gay, but . . .'

'I'm not.'

'You want to talk?' Pete says. He just stood up. 'Because you're really, really acting insane. It's like you're not here. It's like you're not you.'

'I don't know.'

'If you want to give me a blow job, just do it,' he says. I

think he's angry. 'Why are you making such a big fucking deal out of it?'

'What were you going to tell me?'

That or something else I did or said makes him hit me in the shoulder. 'Oh, Christ,' he says. 'No fucking way.' Then I guess he starts to leave.

'Don't, okay?'

My mom just knocked, and said there was an Oriental here to see me. She knows his name. Names go, then who, then any logic, then the world I understand. I've stopped stressing out about why Pete took off, and what he'll tell everyone about me, but it's taken a couple of beers and concentration.

'Yeah, come in.'

Tran's wearing this pair of black pants I said I liked when I was drunk. I guess I still do, or just the rear. It's the ice skater thing, and my beer.

'Here.' I hand him one.

'You changed your room,' Tran says, walking around. He's doing that so I'll get every view of his ass, and he hasn't started drinking.

'No, I didn't.'

I guess he doesn't know what to say about that, and sits down on my bed. 'Well, something's different,' he says.

I'm driving somewhere that I haven't decided. I could find Gilman's street, or make a U turn, and take the freeway. I could find Jude's cabin, or that motel from last night. Tran's drinking his second beer, so he's wasted. It doesn't take much. He keeps almost passing out, then barely opening his eyes. The world's not worth it. We're practically at the hill. The street has broken up into gravel, then turned into dirt. It stops all cars dead

at a gate, where you can pull off and park. I just did, and tried
to start something with Tran. I couldn't tell if he liked it, or if
that was his beer, and my beer made the rest of it up. So that got
me upset. My being upset woke him up, and he suddenly opened
his door. I had to grab him to get that to stop.

'It's Larry.' I just fished Tran's cell phone out of his pocket. First
I punched him a couple of times, and he's quiet.

'What do you want?' Gilman says. I think I can hear the
outdoors making noises around him. They have a backyard.

'You know that guy Tran?'

I guess Gilman thinks about that. 'I know who he is,' Gilman
says.

'I'm with him right now, and I'm kind of confused.'

'Look, this vigilante shit,' Gilman says. He can't go on. It must
confuse him. After Pete left, I read more of the notebook. The
Gilman part's vague, but I think I know why the boy's dead, and
Pete's next. But I need to make sure.

'I don't know what to do.'

'What do you mean you're with him?' Gilman says.

'We're sitting in my car.'

'What do you want me to do about it?' Gilman says. 'Why are
you calling me?'

'I don't know. I need a rationale.' He likes that word. If you
look at his website, it's there about five thousand times. I don't
think he understands it.

'Look, I don't like bugs, okay,' he says. 'But I don't know
the guy.'

'What's there to know?' It's all in the way I said that. Then I
wait.

'Okay, fuck, where are you?' Gilman says.

*   *   *

I've dragged Tran off the road, and down a slope. I made him walk at first, but he fell down and started to yell, so I hit him again. He sounded more like a dog, so we're safe. I took his pants off, and threw them as far away as I could. He's where and how I laid him. This isn't how I ever wanted to do it, or with whom, but I'm trying again. It still won't work, but I hit him really hard in the head that last time. So I'm practically alone, and I don't think it counts.

Gilman gets close enough to see us, and stops. I heard him coming, and quit what I was doing in time. 'Fuck,' he says. 'You fucking idiot.'

'I'm really confused.'

I guess Gilman looks at Tran long enough to see his back move, then crouches down to make sure. 'Okay, what's going on?'

'I don't know.'

'What are you asking me to do?' he says.

'Do you think I'm gay?'

'Fuck, I don't know,' Gilman says.

'Do you think if I don't kill him, I am?'

He has to think about that. 'Did you really not read the notebook?' he says.

'I read parts.'

'I guess I'd say don't do it,' he says. First he shut his eyes tight. 'Because I understand, but I don't think that's a good enough reason.'

'What if I just rape him?'

'That's probably better,' he says, and hugs himself. He takes a deep breath, and slowly lets it out. 'So what's wrong with him?'

I pull Tran's hair. His head lifts, but nothing else happens.

'Fuck,' Gilman says. He looks at me, and I can tell he's upset that I know. Then there's nothing to say, or it's too complicated for him.

'He's gay.'

'Oh,' he says. 'I hate gay people.'

'Yeah.'

'I could go off on the whole thing with the Nazis,' he says. 'They did some really sick things.'

'They weren't gay.'

'Well, that isn't why they did it,' he says. 'Or those Matthew Shepard guys. They had girlfriends.'

'See, this is why I wanted you to come.'

'So did you really burn the notebook?' Gilman says. He just raped Tran, and is pulling up his pants. He started the rape on his knees, then slid his hands underneath Tran and pretended there were breasts. Then he looked angrily at me, and lay down on Tran's back, and whispered some swear words. So I'm confused now.

'Yeah.'

'If you kill him afterwards, I won't say anything,' he says. He means after my turn raping Tran. But I'm not gay, and deciding how to tell him. When I saw how he acted, I knew. I don't give enough of a shit about Tran to pretend he's a girl. That's different.

'Or you could do it.'

'That's true,' he says. I just handed him the gun.

'Then you'd know if you were gay.'

Gilman just grabbed my arm and tried to pull me off Tran, but he couldn't. He didn't fire the gun. I couldn't make him. Maybe he tried to explain his rationale, and I lost it. I was hitting Tran, but Gilman stopped me.

'Is everyone allright?' some voice yells, maybe again. It's coming from up on the hill. I didn't hear any cars, but I forget people walk.

'Yeah,' Gilman yells.

I start to hit Tran again, but Gilman grabs my arm.

'What's going on down there?' the voice yells.

'Fuck off,' Gilman yells. He's holding my arm really tight, so I'm coming around to the world.

'Let go.'

'Larry,' Gilman whispers. 'Fucking Jesus.'

'Well, keep it down,' the voice yells. Then I guess whoever yelled at us walks away, because some leaves crunch. They're far away from us like the stars.

'What?!'

'What the fuck are you doing?' Gilman says. I guess he means why am I yelling and why was I punching the ground. Tran isn't there anymore. I can see that.

Gilman's taken off, and I'm driving. The gravel just rehardened into a street. There aren't any houses around, just foundations for ones in the future. Tran is limping in my headlights, and turned to look. His face is fat and badly shaped on one side, and there's a big dot of blood on his dirty underpants. When he sees it's my car, he sits down on the curb.

'Hey.' I rolled down the window first. I don't know what else.

'What just happened?' Tran says.

That takes me a second. 'Gilman caught us having sex, and I had to pretend I was beating you up.'

Tran looks up at me for a weirdly long time, then starts crying. He has a high pitched and nasal bug voice, so it's intense.

I hold his pants and shirt out the window. He doesn't see that at first, until I shake them and yell. 'Come on. Hurry.'

*   *   *

My mom's passed out drunk in a chair. I saw her body from the back. Her TV show has turned into some news program she'd never watch. Dad's easily in bed by now, and Jim probably crashed. His door is unlocked, because I tried the handle. I just called Jude to give myself and him a chance.

'I was asleep,' she says. I just reminded her about our thing for tonight, and explained why I'm late. I left some parts out. I just need her to say it.

'Please, Jude. I'm really confused.'

She lets that sit, and I guess thinks. I'm too tired now to feel out the silence. Or else everyone and everything's tired except me.

'I should go back to sleep,' she says.

'I really think I'm going to do something sick.'

'Larry,' she says, or more like starts. It doesn't go anywhere for a second. 'Pete's here.'

I know what that means. If I hadn't left the gun in my car, I'd kill myself right now, so she could hear it. 'So you're in love with him?'

'So I know you're gay,' she says. 'So fuck off.'

When I stopped getting drunk, I turned into a liar. That's the only way I could stop. I told everyone I hit Rand because he did something gay to Jim. I didn't think he actually did until those naked pictures showed up and confused me. I didn't think about what I was feeling for Jim until Rand confused me. I think when I hit him, and maybe the boy or even Tran, I was trying to kill myself out of shock. I don't know if Rand was lying. I don't know if Jim's just an innocent victim, or if Rand made that up. I don't know or else want to know if I raped Jim those times, or if Rand only saw it that way because he was gay and I'm not. I don't know if Jim feels suicidal without me, or if the boy wrote that down in his notebook because he was suicidal and thought everyone was like him. I don't know if the boy really wanted to die, or just felt depressed about everything for a minute. I know I should read the whole notebook again right this second. I just can't.

I'm standing by Jim's bed. He was asleep, or almost. Maybe I shook him. He used to wake up suddenly at the wrong times of night, and come into my bedroom. That's what started it. He'd say he was upset, and just wanted to talk. I loved that part. It's been a long time. I came in here wanting to tell him the truth about killing the boy, until I saw him asleep. Then I wanted to say I was sorry I raped him those times, if I did, but when he woke up, I couldn't. Now I want to do both or neither. I can't tell.

'What's the matter?' he says.

'Nothing.'

'What's that?' he says. I was reading a book about ghosts to calm down. That didn't work, and it's still in my hand.

'I don't know.'

He turns on this little lamp by his bed. So I hand him the book. When he sits up, the sheet falls down, and I can see that he's naked. It's a book about communicating with the dead. That and maybe Jim are all I care about understanding these days.

'I saw Dr. Thorne.'

'Mom told me,' he says.

'I didn't know you were going to him.'

'Yeah,' Jim says.

'So what does it mean?'

Jim checks in with me. I'm looking down at his stomach. He looks there, but doesn't know what I'm seeing. Otherwise, he wouldn't put the book down and lie back, so I can look really close. 'I don't know,' he says in this soft voice. I can't describe it.

'Yeah, you fucking do.'

*   *   *

I guess I dragged Jim off the bed, and strangled him on the floor, but I've stopped. He's on one side, coughing and holding his mouth to be quiet. I'm on my knees beside him. I don't think he yelled, or I'd know. Whenever I realize how much I used to worry about him, I always lose it. I used to drive to a rifle range somewhere and shoot off my guns. When my dad confiscated them, I'd get drunk.

'Larry,' he says. 'What's the matter?'

'Don't.'

'Okay,' he says. He sits up and yanks one of the sheets off his bed, then pulls it over himself. So I pull it off him, and he starts to cry. He can't control anything when he cries, so it's scary to see. He can't help that.

'I'm sorry.' I mean for always doing what he wanted me to do, if that's true. It's so confusing. When I pulled off the sheet, I wanted to put it back on. So I do.

'What's wrong?' he says.

'Nothing.' I yelled that, so he looks at the door. You can't hear people walk in this house, because the carpet's so thick. But I guess Mom doesn't care if I'm upset, or she'd already be here. 'Just fucking say it.'

'Larry,' Jim says.

'Don't.'

'Don't what?' he says, and start to cry even harder. It's more like he's wailing. I just pulled the sheet off him again.

'I don't know.'

3.

I'm on my back, and feel unusually honest. It's the first time I've been so upset that I can't sit and fight. Maybe his eyes or whole face are the cold, but he isn't. I think the ceiling's been painted some psychological color. We only have an emergency minute before school. Jim's waiting for me in the lobby. It's just a few feet away from here, if that. So I hope the walls are thick. They don't look it.

'Okay. I've been lying a lot.'

'Give me an example,' Dr. Thorne says.

'I thought I killed someone last night, but I didn't.'

'You thought you did,' he says.

'Yeah, but he's not dead. And other things. I said I had sex with someone, but I didn't.'

'You used the word thought,' he says.

'I meant lie.'

That takes him a second. 'Do you know why you're lying?' he says.

'I guess to not think about things.'

'How did it go with your friend in the car?' he says.

'That was a lie too.'

'So tell me what was real?' he says.

'I don't know. Not much. Like Jude doesn't love me. That's a big one. I thought Pete was gay. I thought this other guy I sort of know was gay. And another guy, too. I thought I was gay, but I'm not.'

'Your friend who died was gay,' he says.

'I think so.'

'You weren't responsible for his death,' he says.

'I know. Everyone says that.'

'Do you think you were?' he says.

'I thought I wasn't, but then I realized I was.'

'When did you realize that?' he says.

'The other night.'

That takes him a second. 'Do you know what's true?' he says.

'Yeah, sometimes I do.'

'Tell me something that's true,' he says.

'Is Jim suicidal?'

That takes him a second. 'Do you think he is?' he says.

'If someone's going to die anyway, is it wrong to kill him?'

'Yes, it is,' he says. 'But you didn't kill your friend.'

'I know all these people who are going to die.'

'Like who?' he says.

'Like Jim and my dad, and Rand was going to die, and someone else I know wanted to die. And I think a lot of people at school are going to die.'

'Do you think all of that is true?' he says.

'Yeah, it's true.'

'What about you?' he says. 'Are you going to die?'

'I don't care.'

'Do you want to talk about the other night?' he says.

'I guess.'

'What did your mother see?' he says.

'I wasn't coming out of Jim's room. He wanted me to come in, but I didn't.'

'Why were you naked?' he says.

'Because I was thinking about it.'

'What were you thinking about?' he says.

'All the lies, I guess.'

That takes him a second. 'Would you object to going back on the anti-depressant?' he says.

'I guess not.'

'Can I ask you one more thing about the other night?' he says. 'Because our time's almost up.'

'Okay, if it's not about Jim.'

'Then I'll see you on Thursday,' he says.

That shocks me, and I guess I sit up and look directly at him. There are so many other questions. He just has to ask. He's so close to it. He could see it in my eyes if he looked, but he's writing my prescription.

Jim's t-shirt is slightly newer than mine. My jeans are black. I'm tall, and he isn't yet. My hair's brown, and his is more dirty blond. My face is okay, and his face is either mine mixed with Mom's, or confusingly like a girl's when it's dark. Other than that, I always thought we were the same. That's why we should talk now before it gets dark, but I can't. I have to watch the road.

'Are you okay?' Jim says. I guess he finally realized I'm not.

'No.' I don't know where to go next. I mean in words. His school's just ahead, so that's settled.

'What did you tell him?' Jim says.

'Nothing. What do you tell him?'

'I don't want to say because I know you'll get mad,' Jim says.

He looks at me. It's just the side of my head. So we're safe, unless I turn it. We just came to a stop in the school's loading zone, and a car honked behind us. So it's now or not at all.

'I don't want to do that stuff we used to do.'

'Why?' he says, and gets a stranglehold on his backpack.

'I just don't want to.'

Jim grabs the door handle, but doesn't turn it. Then nothing happens and neither one of us moves for what feels like a minute. He starts to say something, then makes an uncomfortable face, and turns the handle.

'Please, Jim.'

'Okay,' he says. I turn my head, but he's outside the car, and is slamming the door.

I hit Rand in the head, and he fell on the floor. He was unconscious for a while, or faked it. That part's true. It's what he said before I hit him. Maybe it was nothing. At first, I thought I'd killed him. So I made up an excuse for why I hit him, to make everyone think he deserved what I'd done. When Rand woke up, he got angry. He told me that I was insane. I'd just tried to explain. I think I couldn't, because of why I'd hit him. So I guess it wasn't nothing. I think I might have taken what he said to me, and reversed it. When he died, maybe the wrong explanation got stuck. When the Franks try to interview ghosts, they don't really answer the questions. They just say what they want. It hardly even matters what they're asked. Maybe if you knew them before, the two do coincide. They only tell you what's bothering them. I just felt like Rand would be bothered by what's wrong with me, and could have straightened it out.

'What?' I just looked in Sam's eyes, and saw the shit. He's a guy my age who works part time at the drugstore. I've been at parties with him. They're usually drunk.

'No offense,' he says. He just looked up my history in the computer, and noticed Jim's above mine.

'What is all that shit?'

'Mostly anti-depressants,' he says. 'That one's a sedative. Those two are anti-psychotics. So's that one.'

I look at the list, while he fills my prescription. I'm using that trick the boy used to make sense of the stars, but it's hard when you don't want to know, or maybe already do. 'What?'

'I said you know him, right?' he says, and hands me a flyer. I guess it came off a stack. Luckily, it's an older school picture, so the boy isn't quite himself. So I honestly don't.

'What's going on?' I've joined Will and Tran in our usual spot. First I made myself cold. I don't think I can do it for long. I saw Tran's black eye and swollen cheek from far away, so I'm looking at Will.

'I don't know,' Will says. 'There's a bunch of bullshit.'

'You mean about the freak disappearing.'

'Yeah, that, too,' he says.

'I broke up with Jude.'

'Yeah,' Will says. 'I guess I talked to her.'

'She's telling everyone you're gay,' Tran's voice says.

I'm still successfully cold. 'I can't believe it.'

'I told Will it wasn't true,' Tran's voice says.

'And that you're in love with Pete Hampton,' Will says.

I just looked at Tran. I don't care if it seemed like a natural shift. His face has been through something rough, and looks more bug than it usually does, but his eyes aren't so different. 'What happened to you?'

'I walked into a tree,' Tran says.

'And that you had sex with your brother,' Will's voice says.

'Okay.' I stood up and yelled that. I didn't plan it. So now

I'm walking away, and everyone's looking at me, if they already weren't.

School's down the street, not that far. I'm in front of the 7-11, drinking a Coke. I needed it so I could take the first anti-depressant. It's down. I don't remember it making a difference. I might have lied to everyone that it did. Then Tran joined me, and asked for a sip. We'll hear the bell.

'Okay, remind me what happened last night.'

'Why?' Tran says. He holds the Coke can an inch away from his mouth, and pours some inside. His upper lip's swollen and pussed, so that's him being nice to us both.

'Because I forgot.'

'Gilman Crowe caught us having sex,' Tran says.

'No, I mean the lie.'

'That is the lie,' he says. 'You thought I was gay, and when I wouldn't have sex with you, you beat me up and let Gilman Crowe rape me.'

I almost hit him. 'No, I didn't.'

'Okay, I walked into a tree,' he says, and hands me the Coke. I guess it was more like a shove.

'So that's mine?' I can't look, but he'll know what I mean. There's only one awful thing about him that belongs to me now. It could have been so different.

'Most of it,' he says. 'I really did walk into a tree.'

'That's funny.'

'But then I guess that's your fault,' he says.

Last night I read the boy's notebook from cover to cover. I'd been avoiding certain parts. I wanted to hear it from Rand. The dead talk in mysterious ways, from what I've seen on TV. If you knew them before, you can supposedly feel what they mean. If you didn't, it just gives you the chills and sounds like lyrics. The boy wrote about everything like a reporter. There's no escaping it. He really liked Jim and me, and just says that. Everything Jim said to him about me, he just repeats. That goes for what I said to him too. So I guess he's the one who is telling the truth, and I should burn it.

'Okay, what?' Gilman says. He said something before that. It's already smoke. I just stole him away from the Nazis. We're stopped dead between a couple of cars in the handicapped lot. It's the only place at the school where they haven't put cameras.

'I want to join your group.'

He looks intensely at me. 'Why?' he says. 'Or do I even want to know.'

That takes me a second. 'You know why.'

'Fuck,' he says angrily, and sits down on the lot. I guess it burns his ass, and he gets right back up. He hardly eats, because he thinks it makes him look German. I guess his chest looks like a bunch of crossed swords. I read that in the notebook.

'I'm sorry I called you.'

'I'm not saying that,' he says. Then he crouches, then waves me down into a crouch.

'But the thing is, I did call.'

'Well, I'm glad you did,' he says, and waves me down harder. 'But I mean, shit.'

'It's confusing.'

'It depends on how you think about it,' he says angrily, I guess because I won't crouch.

'So how do you look at things like that?'

'I don't,' he says.

As soon as he says that, I crouch. I can't explain it. Maybe

I'm just lonely. 'That's why I want to join the group. That's the whole point.'

'I don't know if you remember.' I'm on a pay phone, and just bailed on a class halfway through. I was too complicated for it. I've already laid myself out. I mean in so many words.

In the ear piece, there's a stoned, coughing sound that I think is the guy I called asking a question. His name's Steve, and it's been a long time.

'Rand's friend.'

'Right,' he says. 'What's going on?'

'Tall guy.'

'I know.' If he knew me, he'd say something else. I'm the guy who hit his brother. It's not like everyone in the world doesn't know that. 'You need something?'

'The guy you said looked like a hippie.'

'You need something or not?' he says.

'Yeah, whatever. Shit.' I know how to get there, and climb over the fence. I did it eight thousand times. I just need to know when.

I'm talking to Pete. It's the same phone, but my hand's cupped around it. Some vaguely familiar blonde girl is behind me, reading a book about ghosts while she waits. It's on my shelf. So I'm trying to remember.

'I'm sorry,' Pete says again. It was more of a groan. He's drunk, so I guess that means for everything he ever did. My mom gets like that.

'I know. Hold on.' Then I look at the girl. 'That's a great book.' I just remembered how I know her, and that I was drunk at her house with some friends when I did. I think we kissed.

She seems deep in the book. I miss that. She's also pretty, so it's harder to tell. 'I just started it,' she says, then looks nervously at the big, faded bulldog. That's the only interesting view from the phone.

'Can I call you?'

She tries not to smile, or maybe laugh. We might have even fucked, or I tried. 'Okay,' she says.

'Cool.' Then I smash my mouth into the cupped hand. 'Gilman wants me to kill you, and I'm going to.'

'Yeah, well, . . . ,' he says.

First I wait. 'Tell me why I shouldn't.'

'I'm sorry,' he says. So I guess he either didn't understand me or care. Knowing him, it might be both mixed together. I don't care.

'Yeah, I'm sorry, too.'

Jude's standing near the bulldog with Grace and Marina. All I know about them is they take Ecstacy and go out dancing. So they're the opposite of her. Jude thinks they're boring, or said that once. The girls saw me first. I could see everything she'd told them about me in their faces. Grace supposedly thinks I'm an interesting guy, so that's how I can tell. Jude's back was turned, so I waited. The girls just said something about me to her and walked off, but she's still turned and watching them leave.

'I don't know what to say.'

'I want you and Pete to get it out of there,' her voice says quietly. I know it's just a bunch of scraps and not the boy anymore. So I don't know why that upsets me.

'It?' I guess that sounded angry.

'Just take it out of there,' her voice says. 'And put it somewhere else.'

'And then what?'

'Then kill yourself or be gay,' her voice says. 'I don't care.'

Then she turns around, and faces me, but had to fold her arms first. 'Did Pete tell you?'

'Tell me what?'

'That prick,' she says.

This is hard. 'I know you love me.'

'You're psychotic,' she says too loudly. Then she looks around. 'You both are.'

'Yeah, well, you're both dead.' I mean that, but I guess she doesn't get how deep I am anymore. Or her eyes don't, or mine can't tell.

I can't believe I remember this movie. It was already old when I saw it. An actor my age played this guy who'd gone insane on maybe drugs, but was trying to be sane. He was with some sane friends when his insane friends showed up. They yelled his name. He walked half way to them, then got confused. I think they weren't the point. So he sat down right there in the middle. I mean he left his future direction to them. I think his sane friends liked him more, but his insane friends didn't think before they did anything. So they got to him first. That might have just happened to me, but not exactly. At the end of the movie, the guy had gone so insane he pulled a gun on his dad. His dad killed him in self-defense, and it was tragic for everyone he'd ever known. It won't be like that for me.

Steve sells drugs out of a tree house. Their parents' backyard is very wooded and huge, so it's a secret if you're quiet. He used to be Rand's older brother by a year. It's a rich neighborhood, so Gilman's going off about it. He's just saying things he thinks Harris or Kliebald would say. Maybe they posted words like these on their website. So I guess he's not technically thinking. It's just some boring bullshit about liberals' fucked up respect for the wrong kinds of people. But I'm trying not to think it too far, and nod along like a Nazi.

'So I read the boy's notebook.'

'You said,' he says. That stopped him. I really tried not to. 'I can just imagine what he wrote.'

'I didn't know you knew him.'

'Okay, what did he write?' Gilman says, and slumps down the seat. 'No, wait, I don't want to know.'

'It was just some emotional stuff about you.'

'Me,' he says.

'What he felt about how you acted with him.'

'I wasn't like anything with him,' Gilman says. 'I just explained the group.'

'He was a deep guy.'

'I felt like he wasn't listening to me,' Gilman says.

'He had this weird thing where he would look at the stars, and imagine they were the lights of a city, and think about what kinds of people would live there. It's like he knew he couldn't understand the stars. So I guess what you said was like that.'

'Okay, what did he write?' Gilman says.

'Basically, that you were lonely.'

'Yeah, well, then he was out of his mind,' Gilman says. 'What a fucking bullshit, stupid thing to say. That's not deep.'

'You saw him naked, right?'

'Whatever,' Gilman says.

'You know all those scars on his body? His mom used to sell him to gay guys, and they beat him up, and did sadistic gay shit to him. Then he started doing things like that to himself.'

'I don't care,' Gilman says.

'I think he wanted people to look at them like he looked at the stars, and think about what kind of person would live in that body.'

'What the fuck are you saying?' Gilman says.

'That he wanted to die, so what we did to him doesn't matter.'

'I didn't do anything,' Gilman says.

'Well, you paid Pete to kill him.'

'Yeah, but he didn't, you did,' Gilman says. I wasn't looking at him, but we've just stopped at a light. He was already looking at me. So it's intense.

'That's your rationale.'

'Think about it,' he says.

'Oh, Larry,' Steve says. He's heavier set than when Rand was alive, with much longer, wrecked hair. The three of us almost fill the treehouse, sitting in corners. There's some shit that Steve sells on the floor. The door is just a smelly blanket, and the building's been warped out of shape by the rain.

'How's it going? This is Gilman.'

'Yeah,' Gilman says.

'How psycho,' Steve says, and laughs. I guess he's either stoned, or his eyes are remembering something I don't, or see differently. It looks warmer for him.

'It's weird, yeah.'

'Well, so, Jesus,' Steve says. 'I didn't think you smoked.'

'I don't.'

Steve's still glazed over, and glances at Gilman. 'You smoke?' he says.

'No,' Gilman says.

'I've been thinking a lot about Rand.'

'Yeah, sure,' Steve says. 'It doesn't end.' He has a joint out, and lights it. I guess Gilman hates drugs, and looks angrily at me.

'So you remember I hit him.'

I can see Steve's eyes hunting his past, and that they haven't caught up with that moment, or at least how I see it. He's still too warm.

'He never told you about that?'

'Yeah,' Steve says. 'I'm just remembering. I kind of blocked all that out.'

'Did he tell you what happened?'

Steve looks at Gilman. 'What's your story?' he says.

'No story,' Gilman says.

I guess that takes Steve a second. 'Yeah, I remember,' he says.

'So what did he say?' Then I punch the treehouse wall. Steve was starting to talk, but he either stopped, or what he did say was short.

'What is this?' Steve says nervously, looking at us both.

'I'm losing my shit. That's what's happening.'

'I didn't know,' Steve says.

'What did Rand say?'

'Give him a second,' Gilman says.

'Tell me.' I yelled that, so it's quiet. No one says anything, so I take the smelly blanket, and rip it down from its nails.

'You guys should take off,' Steve says.

'Let's go,' Gilman says to me. Then he gets up on one of his knees, and looks over at Steve. 'You don't have any guns for sale?'

'I sell pot, dude,' Steve says.

'What did he fucking say?' I yelled that, too, and did something with the blanket. I can't feel what. I guess it ripped at some point in whatever I did.

'All he said was you guys had a fight,' Steve says, and looks at Gilman. 'What's the matter with Larry?'

'I don't know,' Gilman says. 'I hardly know him.'

*   *   *

In the notebook, the night I hit Rand, he came by my house without being invited. No one was home except for Jim, so he said Rand could wait in my room. Rand looked through my stuff for anything he could sell to buy drugs, and found some notes Jim had written to me. Rand freaked out, I guess, and asked Jim about them. Jim denied everything, and told Rand not to tell me. Rand got upset about that, and yelled at Jim until I guess he confessed about us. I don't know he described it. When Rand confronted me, I was already sick of how stoned and obnoxious he'd gotten, and told him the truth. I guess I said some terrible things I didn't mean about Jim. Jim was listening outside the door, and heard me say them, and maybe misunderstood. When Rand came to, I thought he got up and left. I was upset, and took off in my car. But in the notebook, he went to Jim's room. He told Jim I was sick, and threatened to call the police. After Rand left, Jim felt so confused about everything that he took enough sleeping pills to kill him, but they didn't. That was the second time. In the notebook, Jim was in love with me then. I don't know if he is anymore. That's probably what confused him. That's probably why he keeps trying to kill himself over and over. I know that's not clear. I think I always felt that from Jim, and it made me insane. If I'd known I would end up insane, I would have hit Rand hard enough to kill him right then. When I realize Jim loved me, I want to kill myself and him. I can't help it. I want to kill Jim, then kill myself. If I'd been Rand, I would have killed Jim and me. But I killed the boy instead of us, because that's more how I am. I never do what I want. The only way I'll keep from killing Jim, or else he'll keep from killing himself, is if I'm dead. Because I want to hit Jim like I hit them. I mean Rand and the boy, especially. I want to hit him so hard, he'll die. I can't stand that I want him to love me like that, and I wish he'd just kill himself for good. It's so confusing. I think I'm going to kill him, if he doesn't love me anymore. I can't believe it. I'm going to tell him I love him either way, then kill both of us if he doesn't. I don't understand it. I don't care if he's my brother.

'What's your problem?' Gilman says. I'm driving him home. The world's such a lie. I guess I'm driving down the street like it doesn't even matter.

'You are.' When I said that, I turned a corner so suddenly that he had to grab onto the seat.

'You know what?' he says. 'You can't be in the group.'

'Fine, then I'll just tell everyone you're gay.'

'Think about it,' he says. I guess he means about who'll believe who. That's it. I hit the brakes, which throws him into the dashboard.

'I didn't burn the notebook.'

'Fuck off,' he says. Then he sort of pulls himself upright, and opens the passenger door. So I kick him all the way out.

'Think about it.'

I found the first pay phone, and stopped. It's in a gas station. My car door is open, and the keys are still in the ignition. That's in case Gilman walks by. I'm not far from where I dumped him. But hopefully he broke one or both of his legs when I kicked.

'How can I help you?' says a man's voice. It's maybe Texan. I've been transfered to him. So I had time to work on perfecting a stupid high voice, if I have.

'I know who killed that missing boy.'

'Okay, hold on for one moment,' his voice says, and maybe writes something down.

'I can't.' My voice feels incredibly fragile.

'What's your name?' his voice says.

'Tran. I don't know my last name. I'm too upset. I was raped. I'm Oriental.'

That takes him a second. 'Do you know your assailant?' his voice says.

'He's a Nazi. It doesn't matter. I know who killed that boy.'

'So you know your assailant?' his voice says again.

'Yeah. I mean no. I mean what do you mean?' I just lost the stupid voice, and it's mine. So I'm punching the phone.

'Try to stay calm,' his voice says.

'Gilman Crowe, okay? Just fucking arrest him.'

When I finally get home, some reporter is there. She arrived with the Franks. I guess they phoned earlier, and Mom drunkenly gave them directions. The reporter is profiling them for a paranormal-themed magazine I sometimes read. That's all I know. She's somewhere with Jim, so I'm nervous. No one knows why. The Franks are both heavy-set, and wear tight red t-shirts with their website address on the front. I just got them away from my mom, and locked us inside my room. They're sitting on my bed, but I can't. They just noticed the picture of Rand on my dresser. It's from two years ago, so I don't know if it counts. Rand wasn't on drugs yet, and not anything else that made me hit him.

'It's very sad,' Mrs. Frank says to her husband. It's true. If you look at that picture, and think of Rand dead, the thought kills itself before he's dead. By the time he was dead, he already looked it to me. All he had to do was close his eyes.

'He was cool.' I don't know what else to say on that front. Looking at that picture, I guess he and I were incredible friends once.

'You miss him,' she says.

'Yeah.' That's true, but the way I whispered it was for them.

'Do you ever sense him in here?' he says.

'I don't know what you mean.'

'Oh, he's here,' she says.

My room is covered with shit I used to like. It's scary looking, or I thought so then. It seems so easygoing, compared to what's scaring me now. The Franks are too old to realize what is softcore or not, so maybe they've picked up on that.

'Why would he want to come here?'

Mr. Frank goes off about how the dead are more insect than human. They have no brains or hearts, and the things they used to know back when they were alive are like magnets.

'Maybe you should try over there.' I point at the floor between my bed and the dresser.

'That's interesting,' he says to her.

'That's where we felt him,' she says. But she nods at the picture of Rand. It's framed and brownish from never having been cleaned, and tilts back on the wall like it has fallen asleep it's so bored of my life. I used to think that was depressing.

I'm in the hall, on the phone. I gave the Franks a list of questions for Rand, then left before they unfolded the paper. I tried to write in code, but you can tell Rand was gay and I'm not. My left ear holds Jude. My right ear is trying to hear what Jim and the reporter are saying. His door's closed, but I just walked into the bathroom.

'I don't know, Larry,' Jude says. I think she's crying. She means if Pete's at home, or what he might confess to someone, he's so drunk.

'Do you love me?' That was a whisper. I'm back to caring, or wanting to know I can fuck her, and worried I wouldn't love her if we fucked. It might have been that blonde girl.

I guess the reporter and Jim aren't sitting on or very close to Jim's bed, because what they're saying just sounds like a room.

'What?' Jude says. 'Jesus Christ, who cares?'

'I mean I know you do, but I need to hear it.'

'Larry, this is fucking serious,' she says.

'Do you love me?'

Jim's room just went quiet. So I guess I yelled that.

'Larry?' Jim's voice says. I can tell it's from his bed.

'Look, just please get it away from the cabin,' Jude says. 'Are you nuts?'

'It's my brother,' Jim's voice says, I guess to the reporter.

This is hard. 'I love you.' I guess I do, no matter who hears me. I know I said it loudly enough.

'What?' Jude says. I don't care why.

Then I wait and wait, but Jim doesn't say anything for so long that I kick and punch the wall.

'You heard me.'

The graveyard's full of stars from the black and white days. You can find them with a map. It's also full of people my age who don't seem to know anyone here. There's something dead on Rand's grave that might have been flowers. It could have blown from somewhere else, or the people my age might have kicked it. The Franks are squinting distance away, interviewing the ground, and the reporter is watching with us on the grass.

'Do you believe in them?' It probably sounds like I mean in the dead, but I meant in the Franks. I guess either answer's okay.

'Honestly?' says the reporter. She's maybe in her thirties, and overly tan with blonde hair and crowsfeet to her ears.

I wait and wait. 'Forget it.'

She only cares about Jim. He's sitting close to her right. 'You feel okay?' she says to him, and rubs his shoulder.

'Sleepy,' he says, and yawns.

'Come here,' she says, and tips him over into her lap. His head,

I mean. She adjusts it with her hands so he's comfortable. Then he smiles up at her, which I can't believe.

'He's a liar.' That just blurted out of me.

'Who is?' she says.

'I didn't tell her anything,' Jim says. I'd just pointed down at him, so she'd know who I meant.

'Now I'm intrigued,' she says, and looks at me.

'You're not his fucking mother.' I guess I yelled that, because the Franks raise their microphone off the ground.

'Larry,' Jim says. He was lying on his side, but he rolls over onto his back, and looks up intensely at me from her lap.

'What are you doing, Jim?' I yelled that, too. So now everyone's looking at me, even the guys and their girlfriends my age who think cemeteries are cool.

'This isn't my fight,' the reporter says, and does this thing with her hands. It's like she's brushing me off, or what I'm feeling. My mom does that.

'Get off him.'

'Excuse me?' she says.

I'm up on my feet now. I had to get farther away from Jim's face. But now I'm so far away, I feel like I could cry.

'Larry,' Jim says again.

'What.'

My leg just clipped a gravestone and maybe broke. I tried to keep running, then fell on the grass and grabbed my calf. The pain's not so fierce that I can't see the world. Jim is running towards me. He's all gangly. I can't tell if the pain's made me more insane, or if just lying down on my back makes me honest.

'Are you okay?' he says. He just got here, and knelt.

'No.' I'm still crying, but the pain's turned it into yell.

'Do you want an ambulance?' he says.

'No, where are they?' I lift my head and look, but the pain in my leg makes me slam down again. 'Are they coming over?'

'Yeah,' Jim says, after looking back to check.

'Did you and Rand have sex?'

'No,' he says. First he folded his hands on his knees and looked down. So I can't just believe him.

'You did.'

Jim bunches his hands. I mean so tightly together they fill with this really harsh color, and his arms are sort of trembling. 'No, we didn't.'

'Tell me.'

'Maybe you should shut up,' he says, and looks behind him.

I can hear the Franks' clanking equipment. So they're close enough to hear us, and I guess the reporter is too. 'I need to know.'

'Shut up,' Jim says. He looks back once more, and puts his hand on my calf. 'I'm sorry,' he adds. Then he grabs it as hard as he can.

'Fuck.'

My lower leg's only bruised, but no one thinks I can drive. I was out of it when they decided. So the Franks are driving Jim in my car, and I'm shotgun beside the reporter. I guess she's writing another article about guys in high school and depression. That was her thing about Jim. It's related to Columbine. She's read so many books that she can see depressed guys like we're ghosts. We don't have to move. We don't even have to talk to her first. She says my problem is rage mixed with some bigger word, so I don't interest her. That's not her thing. At first I was thinking she'd save me from Jim if she used the right words, but he's too complicated so far. That's her thing. I know that already. So I'm barely listening now. She's just confused about Jim like

I was before Rand confused me more, and I started drinking. I used to care what was wrong with Jim too. He made it seem like what I did to him helped, but I guess I was sick, and it didn't.

'What?' I think the reporter just said something nice. All I heard was the sound.

'I said where do I turn again?' she says.

It doesn't matter. 'The next street, but pull over for a second.'

She looks in the mirror, then slows to the right. My car drives past us. I watch it go until they've turned onto a street that turns into our street after a couple of blocks.

'Just follow them.' Then I open the door, and get out. I think I know where I am.

Patsy's mom opened the door when I knocked, then turned and yelled for her. I didn't remember her name until it was shouted like that. I had a lie for why I didn't call first. Maybe the pain from my leg is doing things to my face, because Patsy looked like she cared. So I lied about how I hurt it. That's all we've been talking about in her room. The story's stupid. Her room looks like my bedroom might look if I hadn't left it scary seeming so Rand's ghost would hang out. I mean it's wall to wall pictures and posters of boys like Jim, but healthier and in rock bands.

'Do you have a younger brother?' she says. We're sitting on her bed. I was there first. I guess she just decided my pain was old news, and changed the subject.

'Yeah, why?'

'That's what I thought,' she says. 'Jim, right?'

It takes me a second. 'Yeah, people like him.'

'What's he like?' she says.

'I don't know. Depressed all the time, why?'

'You can tell,' she says.

'So why were you reading that ghost book?' I guess I expected piles or shelves of them. I can't even see it, or any book.

'It's my dad's,' she says. 'He's a therapist.'

'Oh, right.' I knew there was something that made me not trust her.

'He makes me hang out at his office and read psychology books so we'll bond,' she says. 'They're divorced.'

'Oh, right.'

'But that's how I met your brother, so it's cool,' she says.

'Yeah, we hardly talk.' Then I lie down on my back. It's just a coincidence, or the intimidating walls.

'That's too bad,' she says.

'I'm kind of the reason he's depressed.'

'Do you like folk music too?' she says.

'No, I just make people depressed. Your dad knows all about it.'

'That's too bad,' she says.

'I sort of went insane a few years ago.'

'You go out with Jude, right?' she says.

'I did, but we broke up.'

'I didn't know,' she says. 'I sort of have a boyfriend now.'

'You remember that guy at school who died last year?'

'Yeah,' she says.

'He was my best friend. I think he was in love with me, but I wasn't gay, so he turned into a drug addict. Now all my friends are fucked up guys who are in love with me.'

'So you fell in love with one of them?' she says.

'It's more like I worry I will.'

'Oh, so Jude . . . I get it,' she says.

'Are you in love with your boyfriend?'

'I don't know. It's different,' she says.

'I didn't even love my friend until he was dead. I don't even love my brother.'

'My brother died,' she says.

'That's weird. Mine almost did a few times.'

'I guess that's why my dad made me read about ghosts,' she says. 'Wait, your brother almost died?'

'He tried.'

'I didn't know it was that serious,' she says.

'How did your brother die?'

'He got lost when he was camping and fell off a cliff,' she says, and points at one of the pictures on her wall. 'That's him.'

I turn my head and look. 'He kind of stands out.' It's the same, blown up size as the others. He's blond too, but actually seems like he's looking at someone and cares.

'Yeah, he wasn't that cute,' she says.

'No, I mean he looks like a deep person.'

'He wasn't, really,' she says. 'He just liked to go skiing and camping and stuff.'

'But being into nature can be deep.'

'Is your brother into nature?'

'No, he's into folk music.' I just gave up on her brother, and laid one arm over my eyes. So I guess I'm upset.

'I'm not really into that kind of music, but I like some songs,' she says.

'I'm the one who fucked him up.'

'I'm sure you didn't,' she says.

'I think I did something really bad to him.'

'Really?' she says.

'Yeah, I can't remember. I mean I remember what I did, but

I can't figure out why it was bad. But if it fucked him up this much, I guess it was bad.'

'What did you do?' she says. 'You don't have to say.'

'I just used to hold him sometimes.'

'That's not bad,' she says.

'Maybe it was sexual too.' First I laid my other arm over my eyes.

'Oh, that's not too cool,' he says. 'Does my dad know?'

'It's more like it was sexual for him, but it wasn't for me. I had girlfriends and stuff.'

'That's a really weird thing to say,' she says.

'You mean you think it's bad, no matter what?'

'I don't know,' she says. 'You're making me uncomfortable.'

I sort of hug my head. It's not good. 'I'm sorry.'

'It's okay,' she says.

'I don't know why I told you that. I just thought you liked books.'

'Why, do you?' she says.

'I used to, but they confuse me. Now I'm more into ghosts, because it seems like they would tell you the truth. It doesn't seem like they could lie.'

'My dad doesn't believe in ghosts,' she says. 'He thinks it's ridiculous.'

'Do you?'

'I think I just miss my brother,' she says.

'I know. I miss my friend, too.'

'If Brett was alive, I'd probably think he was a loser,' she says. 'I always thought he was a loser.'

'When my friend died, he was a loser too.'

'Brett just went camping all the time,' she says. 'It was stupid.'

'Rand was a drug addict.'

'I remember,' she says. 'He kind of scared me, but I didn't know him that well.'

'I thought he had sex with my brother. Maybe he did.'

'So is your brother gay?' she says.

'I don't know. I sort of think he is, but I always think everyone's gay.'

'That would be too bad,' she says, and laughs.

'These band guys are probably gay.'

'People always say that,' she says. 'But I guess it doesn't matter. I wouldn't want to be with them anyway. I know they're just stupid guys who want to make money.'

'Would you want to be with Jim?'

'Honestly?' she says. 'Kind of, yeah, except he's too young. What do you mean by "with" him?'

'I don't know. In love.'

'Okay, when I think about him?' she says. 'I'm the only one who understands him, and he realizes that, and falls in love with me.'

'What about sex and stuff?'

'Okay, this is weird,' she says. 'When I think about him, it always ends with just knowing we will, and that it'll be sweet. Does that sound stupid?'

'No, but I'm confused about sex. I think about it all the time, but it's like that part of me is subconscious or something, because I feel like I never think about it. It's hard to describe.'

'I don't really understand what you mean,' she says.

'Okay, don't feel weird, but I came over here because I wanted to fuck you. But I never thought about how could I get you in bed? I think most guys already have plans.'

'I kind of thought you did,' she says, and laughs.

'But I haven't even thought about that.'

'Really?' she says.

'Yeah, I'm just talking to you really honestly, and I almost never do. So I'm mostly thinking why am I doing this? I don't even know you.'

'I guess I've been thinking you did,' she says, 'And I've been thinking what I would do.'

'I do want to. I mean if I could stop talking for a second, and look at you, I really would.'

'That's sweet,' she says.

'But I also think, why? Why would I?'

'Because you like me?' she says.

'Yeah, but do I? Or am I just confused because you're so easy to talk to?'

'Are you sure you're not gay?' she says.

'If I was gay, I wouldn't freak out with guys. I get really upset. I can't even talk about it.'

'Okay,' she says. 'That's interesting.'

'I mean I hit them. I beat them up. I don't even know why I'm doing it.'

'That's not cool,' she says.

'I know, but I can't help it. I think I'm insane.'

'Maybe you shouldn't think so much,' she says. 'My dad would kill me if he heard that.'

'I tried doing that. It's bullshit.'

'You know what I've always liked about you?' she says. 'Even before I knew you were related to Jim?'

'God, I'd love to know.'

'You know that girl Jeanne?' she says.

'Yeah, we used to go out before she was a Nazi.'

'I know, that's so weird,' she says. 'Jeanne told me that when you guys had sex, you would always start to cry. She thought that was sweet. I thought that sounded sweet too.'

'I can get really confused.'

'She says that Nazi Gilman guy does that too,' she says. 'You'd never think he would.'

'He's pretty fucked up, but that's weird.'

'I always liked that you were like that,' she says.

'But I'm not like that anymore. Now I cry all the time. It doesn't take anything. I don't even have to be with a girl.'

'I don't mind if you cry,' she says.

'Yeah, but I can't. I mean thanks, but I feel like I've been crying all day. I think I came here so I wouldn't cry, really. I think I wanted to fuck you, but I guess I just needed to talk.'

'We can keep talking,' she says.

'Yeah, but I can tell it won't help. I should talk to someone who knew me before I lost it, and can tell me what's different. Anyway, you like Jim, and I don't want to think about him right now. And I guess all these pictures are freaking me out.'

'Okay, I'm sorry,' she says.

'That's okay. Maybe you can give me a ride.'

'Sure, if you want,' she says.

'I'm sorry. You're really beautiful.'

'It's okay,' she says. 'I never even thought you would call.'

4.

Rand's family is so together and rich, compared to mine. They have a long, uphill driveway. Their house and front yard are so great they've been in bad horror movies. I got this idea partway home, and Patsy dropped me at the bottom. So when I finally get to the door, my ugly leg's screwing the rest of me up.

'Larry,' his mom says. She's surprised, and hugs me. I used to hate that, but I've thought about her doing it since.

'I'm sorry.'

'No,' she says. 'It's so nice.'

She notices how I'm standing, and lets me sit on a chair just inside. It's the same living room. She looks almost the same, but it's taken extra makeup.

'I'm having a hard time.'

That makes her sit down in a chair, and pay what really seems like incredible attention. I guess that upsets me, and I can't talk.

'We've missed you,' she says finally.

'So, did I kill Rand?'

'No, honey,' she says. 'He had an aneurism. Nothing caused it.'

'You know we fought.'

'I know,' she says. 'He told me. It wasn't that.'

'Do you know why?'

She looks off somewhere, and I guess thinks back on that day for a while. It doesn't make her as warm as I did.

'I mean why we fought.'

'I know what you mean,' she says. I guess it's hard for her to look at me again, but she does. 'Can I show you something?' Then she smiles, but it's like her whole body is begging me to say yes.

I don't know. 'Okay.'

She just got back. I don't know where she went, but I heard someone walking around in Rand's room. It's over my head, and to the right. Maybe they turned the room over to Steve, but it sounded lighter than him. I didn't see it in her hands until she handed it over. It's the kind of photo album you can buy in drug stores.

'Did you know about that?' she says, sitting down again.

'Sort of.' At first, I just knew there was something, and that it kept a secret from me. I had an idea where he hid it, but I was wrong. He only mentioned it twice, and I looked for it once when he was taking a shower. I thought it was drugs, maybe in a box. By the time I found those naked pictures, I'd forgotten. 'You want me to open it?'

'Do you need to open it?' she says.

I guess I need to think about that. I basically know what's inside, but I don't know for sure about seeing it now. But I finger the edge of the album, and look down very hard at the cover. It has a word on it, written in felt tip.

'Those are pictures of Jim,' she says.

'I know.' I guess I do. It wasn't just the word.

'You knew about this?' she says.

'It's sort of why we fought in a way.'

'I haven't told your parents,' she says. 'My husband won't let me, out of concern for your dad.'

Then neither one of us says anything. So I just open the album, and flip through. I can't help it.

'I'd feel more comfortable if you didn't look at it right now,' she says.

'Okay.' But I keep looking.

'I think your mother should know, at least,' she says. I really hate to close the album. I want to go home and stare at them until I remember everything, and can decide. But I don't want her to ask for it back, so I close it.

She's driving me home. They have a Lexus with very low classical music inside. Maybe I'll call her sometime after the album is safe. I have it clamped under my arm, in case she changes her mind. My other hand's on the door in case she asks why I didn't do something to stop it. I guess I did.

'So you found it after he died?'

'What?' she says. Maybe she can't remember the "it." It's pretty far away in our conversation by now. 'No, just before.' Then something new happens suddenly in her eyes, and she looks at me.

'Oh.'

'Sweetie,' she says. Then I guess she thinks about me, or me in combination with everything else. I can see I'm in there. 'Rand committed suicide.'

'Oh.' I have to look out the window. 'How?'

'Here,' she says, and slows the Lexus down until it stops near the curb. We're still in the more hilly, rich neighborhood, so there are a million trees. She puts her car in park, but leaves it running. Then we sit there for a second. 'We always really liked you.'

'I liked you too.' I didn't back then, but I do when I remember them now.

'Rand had a lot of problems,' she says.

'I know.'

'I don't want to blame Jim, but it's hard,' she says. 'My husband blames Rand, but I just can't. I'm his mother.'

'How did he do it?'

'We found an email from Jim,' she says. She looks like she's reading the email again in her mind. It must be intense. 'I realize he's a young boy.'

'I'm really confused.'

'I know you are,' she says. 'I'm being very selfish.'

'I mean always, not just now.'

Then we sit there again. I don't know why I thought she'd want to understand how I feel. She's not my friend.

When I get home, everyone is asleep. My mom actually made it to bed. I have to take the stairs really slowly, because of my leg. She'll leave a note on the stairs if someone called, and she wasn't too drunk. I always hope she'll write something nice, but her notes are just names, sometimes numbers, and when the calls happened, if that. There's no note, but there's a scrap on my bed. It's in Jim's writing, and says to wake him up when I find it, no matter how late. It's been a while since he wrote that. I remember the notes being nicer to me, or imagining they were. I used to keep them, because I thought they meant something, or that the handwriting did. He writes like a girl, and feels sort of like one when it's dark, but I knew he wasn't. Maybe he didn't like that the bedroom always had to be dark, and Rand let it be light, and did things I would only talk about doing to him through a wall. I'm not sure if that's right. I just sat down on my bed, and started looking through the album again. I know I saw some of these pictures, and twisted them into others like these in my head, but I guess they're just upsetting when you know the guy who took them killed himself, and the guy in them hasn't yet.

I didn't have to shake Jim that hard. First I sat down at his computer. It's always on. I found all his old emails, because he once stupidly said his password was my name. There are two from Rand. One's especially old, and just mentions a link to some folk music website. But the last one upset me so much I stood up and shoved my hands into my pockets. They're fists. I don't know what I would have done if I was naked.

'Larry?' Jim says, and tries to see me through the dark. When he does, he sits up holding the covers around him.

'I got your note.'

'Is your leg okay?' he says, and yawns.

'Yeah, it's just ugly and hurts.' I put that foot up on the bed, and raise the jeans leg with my fingers.

'Wait,' he says, and feels around for the knob on the lamp by his bed. It takes him a second. Then he leans close, and one of his hands helps me pull up the jeans so he can see the whole bruise.

'I thought it was broken.'

There's some light on the side of his face, and just enough on the crotch of my jeans. So I know where he's aimed. It was real when I was looking at the pictures. But after what I just read, I had to concentrate on what Jude looks like naked.

'It's not so bad,' he says, and looks at my eyes. He can't seem to do that for long, and looks away at nothing or some confusing thought.

'I don't care.'

I let go of my pants leg, and take ahold of his covers. When he doesn't move or say anything, I pull them off him. I just want to know what he feels. He covers it up with his hands, but not quickly enough.

'Yeah,' he says. 'Who cares?' Then he takes his hands off, and shows me. It's real enough. That'll be the reason, whatever I do.

We're heading toward the mountains. I don't think we'll make it that far. He always asked me to take him away, even to a motel. I guess that could have been me wanting that. It's maybe three in the morning. Since we took off before mom made us breakfast, I'm starting to feel it.

'You hungry?'

'I could eat,' Jim says.

The last time I drove out this way, and felt almost like this, I was pretending that I was with Jim. I think I realize that now. It just took me a couple of days to read and see everything I could about him first.

'This is so intense.' I mean that. He doesn't know how intense.

'We'll see,' he says.

I brought the boy's notebook. It's lodged under my seat. I can't decide when to tell Jim to read it, so I'm counting on some food. I already have a whole story about why I have it, if he asks.

'I mean I hope so,' he says. He means about seeing. Sometimes it just takes him a minute. 'You just seem kind of cold.'

'This okay?' We're pulling into that IHOP. It's less dark outside, and getting lighter not darker. So far that's the only real difference he makes. 'Yeah, you too.'

'Do you think he's alive?' Jim says. He means the boy, and I just mentioned that flyer. I guess I need something that only the notebook can cure.

'No.' I'm studying the menu. So's he.

'Me neither,' he says.

'What do you think happened?'

Jim closes the menu. I guess he figured it out. 'I don't know,' he says, and looks around the restaurant. There are only a few people here, and they're truckers. 'What do you think?'

'I think he wanted to die, so it doesn't matter.'

'You're probably right,' he says, and looks at me. Then we both turn our heads and look out the window at nothing until I just can't anymore.

'I've missed you.'

'Yeah, it's different, though,' Jim says. 'So who were you with when you called me at Bill's?'

'You don't know him. A guy from school.'

'Was it Pete?' he says.

First I wonder how much he understands about that, and can't decide. I know he sneaks into my room. 'No, that's over.'

'Oh, yeah?' he says in this voice without anything I can feel in it.

'That was just some weird trying to find myself thing.'

'Was Bill like that, too?' he says.

'I don't know.'

He's still looking out the window. It can't be about the cars and big, typical sign for the restaurant.

'I think that was more about you.'

He keeps looking out there. 'I like Pete.'

'Fuck you.' Then I laugh.

'I wish you would,' he says, and laughs. It's nice. 'That's mean. I'm sorry.'

'Maybe I will if you shut the fuck up.' Then I look out the window too. There's just nothing out there.

*   *   *

After a while, some insane guy walked into the restaurant, and ordered a coffee to go. He just seemed poor until he started yelling. It was something about UFOs and his brain. The waitress was clearing our plates. She either knew his nickname from before, or thought one up to make us laugh. I didn't. It didn't seem funny.

I just started the car, and Jim laughed again. So I'm upset.

'Your face,' he says. We're already back on the freeway. So I can't see him for long, and must look angry. He won't stop laughing.

'What?'

'It's nothing bad,' he says.

'I think I'm less confused.'

He looks at me, and laughs again. Then he turns on the car's radio. I have it set on a station I liked before Rand died. It plays loud, punching songs that used to help me get angry when I couldn't.

'What's so funny?' Now I guess he's laughing at the music too.

'Okay, you keep looking at me like I'm your girlfriend,' he says.

'See, then you don't understand.'

'Larry,' he says, and laughs. 'I like it.'

'Because I'm thinking, he's my thirteen year old brother. That's all he is.'

'What?' he says, and starts laughing even harder. It's getting ugly.

Jim's reading the notebook. I got even more upset, and pulled it out. He crawled into the back seat with it so I couldn't watch him read. He was sitting up at first, but laid down. I'd have to wreck the car to see him. So I'm listening to him breathe and turn the pages. He's slowed way down. We passed that motel I stayed in with the boy a while back. Now I hardly have any plan left.

'I have to pee.' I don't. I'm just heading off into any rest stop.

'Okay,' Jim's voice says, sounding really tired. I guess he could have been asleep for a while and I wouldn't have known it.

There's another car here, and two huge, long, multi-part trucks. I want to look at Jim, but I think it's too light.

'Aren't you going to pee?' Jim says. We've been sitting here parked for a minute while I wondered what I thought.

'I guess. What about you?'

'I should,' he says.

The bathroom is built out of logs like a cabin. Maybe in twenty-five years, when the trees all around it grow up, that'll work. I always use a stall, and close the door. Jim hasn't peed, or even unzipped his pants. I can't, either. He leaves the bathroom before I stop trying. I thought he would feel what I was feeling, and knock on the door. I even made a fist just in case.

The car looks empty. So I guess Jim's either reading the notebook again or asleep. For a while, he just sat with his eyes shut and thinking. I'm at this vending machine I've been circling around for a while, and bought two Cokes. I have enough pills in my hand to kill Jim. They're my anti-depressants. They're what's left of the original plan. I know they're enough. The doctor said Jim would have died the last time if I hadn't gone into his room when I did. Nobody knows how long I waited. I even threw off the covers, and pushed my ear down on his back to make sure. Then I went in my bedroom and cried until I couldn't kill myself, and woke up Mom.

*   *   *

Jim has been trying to sleep sitting up, or pretending he was. He finally took a drink from the Coke. It's in his hand, which is resting near his crotch. I know he set it there so I'll see what's around it.

'What are we doing anyway?' he says.

'Take a guess.'

'But we obviously aren't doing that,' he says.

'I just need to talk first.'

'What, about how evil I am?' he says.

'I'm evil, too.'

'No, you're not,' he says. 'You're great.' He had to take a drink of Coke, then close his eyes for a second to add that.

'You're the only one who thinks so.'

'Rand thought you were great,' he says.

'Yeah, but he was gay.'

'So are you,' Jim says.

'No, I'm not.'

'Yeah, you are,' Jim says.

'I was just worried about you.'

That takes him a second. 'Then what are we doing?' he says.

'I'm still worried about you.'

That takes him another second. 'You're not even going to try?' he says.

'I am trying.'

'You don't act like it,' he says.

'Well, I'm scared. I'm not like you.'

'Yeah, I'm not scared,' he says.

'So was your whole thing with Rand about me?'

'What thing?' he says.

'Like in those pictures in that fucking photo album.' I guess I yelled that, or at least the last words.

I guess Jim can't say anything, he's so shocked. When he got

Rand's last email, he wrote back begging Rand to at least burn the pictures. That's all. He didn't say don't kill yourself. He didn't say Larry's in love with you too, even though Rand told Jim that was why he was thinking of killing himself. I mean because I wasn't. Jim could have lied. I lie all the time. It's not that hard.

'So, yeah.'

'So, yeah,' he says, and drinks some Coke.

'I think you're what made me insane.'

'Probably,' he says.

'I wanted you to die that night. I sat there on your bed, and waited until I thought you were dead before I told Mom.'

'Why?' he says.

'Because you were making me insane.'

'Is that why you hit Rand?' he says. It was almost a yell. Then he kicks the car floor so hard he has to grab his foot and wince.

'Yeah, that's why I do everything I do. That's why I hit Rand. That's why I only have friends who are gay. That's why I did things I can't even tell you about. You've made so confused.'

'Come on, Larry,' he says.

'What?'

'You're lying,' he says. It was more like a yell. He sits forward as far as the seat belt will let him, and screams so hard it's like he's throwing up his whole life. It could be partly the Coke.

'About what?'

He puts one hand over his eyes, and slugs his head with the Coke. It still sounds pretty full. He knows what him being upset makes me do, and that I can't do anything until we get somewhere dark, and lie down. So I punch him twice not that hard in the side of his head.

'I know Rand killed himself, okay?'

'I'm sorry,' he says, still yelling, just not as hard.

'And I know you didn't stop him.'

'I'm sorry,' he yells again. I had to punch him first.

'It's cool. Just fucking wait.' But I guess I yelled that, so it's not.

We've been driving for a while, and have started up the mountain. I unzipped his pants a few minutes back, and have my hand inside. He liked it, or part of him did, but now it's happening without him. I don't feel anything. I'm just making sure I never did.

'I need to throw up,' he says, and vaguely moves around. He wasn't before.

'I don't want you to.'

He slowly puts his right hand on the crank that'll roll down his window. That's all. Then he sits up straight, maybe to help concentrate. The Coke already fell, and is spilled on the floor.

'Jim.' I guess my hand was too deep in his pants, because I can't pull it out, and we're edging so close to a cliff I can't hit him.

He gives the crank a turn, then shuts his eyes. They were already shut, if you didn't look close.

'Sit back.'

He just hangs there, either dead or almost. I'm only yanking and trying to steer and I guess scared to die.

'Please, Jim.'

We made it as far as a turn off. Then I elbowed his stomach a few times until he sat up, and freed my hand. We're idling in park. I guess some unconscious, more animal part of him opened the door. But he didn't know how to get out. I finally pushed him. His hand got caught under the handle, so most of his body is still in the car. One leg is bent at the knee, and I'm waiting to see if it loses his signal, and falls.

*   *   *

I didn't hear the car until it honked. Jim's leg eventually fell, but I didn't believe that. So I pulled him inside by the legs, and smelled the vomit. I was crying and confused, and had a finger down his throat for a minute. It grabbed me a few times, but that could have been a reflex. Now I either don't care, or realize I can't help.

'Larry?' Jude says. I'm just sitting here now. Jim's either dead, or sitting there not caring if he's dying like me. I can't look anymore. I guess she's seen him, and knows, and can't figure out what to say to me about that.

'Yeah.'

'I have to go,' she says.

'Okay.'

'Pete's at the cabin freaking out. I have to go,' she says.

'Okay.'

'Is he allright?' she says.

'Who?'

'You fucking idiot,' she says. Then I see her walk around to Jim's side of the car. I know his door's still wide open. I think she's touching and looking closely at his face. 'Who is he?'

'What do you mean?'

'You don't want to know, basically,' she says.

'It's Jim.' Then I look over, just in case. He's just incredibly white.

'Jesus, what happened to him?' she says.

'He's been depressed.'

'Hey,' she says. She has his head in her hands, and is shaking it around. 'Hey, hey.'

'Just let him die, Jude. I'm so sick of it.'

Jude shook Jim alive enough to walk with her help, and sit

down on the ground. She's talking to him. He's just nodding or shaking his head, and still holding the notebook. I guess he grabbed it off the seat. There are some trees behind them, and a trail you wouldn't see if you weren't parked that goes into the mountains somewhere. Maybe if you hike for a while, there's a cabin that no one remembers is there.

'Look,' she says. She left Jim sitting by himself, and walked around to my side of the car. I was looking at his confused, cringing face until I couldn't.

'What did he say?'

'He said he got car sick, and he's sorry,' she says.

'That's bullshit. I gave him some pills.'

'I honestly don't care,' she says.

'I just want him to die.'

'You are so mentally ill,' she says. Then she stands up where I can't see her face. 'You want a ride?' she says loudly.

'No.' Then I look at Jim, who I guess was still looking at me. I even mouthed the words I know he wants, then waited for a second. 'You don't.'

I'm standing over Jim. Jude's here too. I'm the one with the painful, weak leg who can't walk very well. We're far enough apart that he'll have to choose between us. If the notebook's the truth, it'll always be me, even when I'm upset. So it's important for so many reasons. Then she'll leave. Then I'll help Jim, or he will help me, walk up that trail, if we can, and maybe hit him as hard as I can in the back of the head so I can't tell who he is.

'I want you to tell her the truth. Then you can go with her if you want.'

'Okay,' he says after staring for a second.

'Just pretend I'm Dr. Thorne or something, and she's not here.'

'No,' he says.

'Then what should I do? What do you want me to do, if I would do anything you wanted?'

'Can I ask you too?' he says.

'That's not fair.' Then I look at Jude. 'See?'

'Why isn't it fair?' she says to me.

'I hate this,' he says, then looks at her. 'Why am I supposed to know?'

'I just want to know what he wants me to do.'

'I don't know,' he says.

'He doesn't know,' she says.

'You told your friend Bill what you wanted me to do.'

'Then why do I need to say it again?' he says.

'For her.'

'I don't care,' she says.

'This is why you're evil, Jim.'

'Okay, what did he tell the Bill guy?' she says to me. Then she looks at Jim. 'What did you say?'

'Tell her.'

'I don't know,' he says. 'I really don't feel good.'

'He told his friend Bill that he was in love with me.'

'That's not what I said,' he says, then looks at Jude. 'Bill just thought everyone was like him. He was crazy.'

That takes me a second. 'Just tell me what you want.'

'I want to sleep for a while,' he says.

'What else?'

'That's all,' he says.

'But that has nothing to do with me.'

'Christ, Larry,' Jude says.

'Yeah, it does,' he says, and looks at her. 'I want Larry to let me sleep for a couple of hours at least.'

'You always do this.'

'That's really what I want,' he says to her.

'Then let's go,' she says to him.

'No.'

Jim holds out one of his arms, so either Jude or I can raise him. We both grabbed it at almost the same exact second.

'Okay, but then you'll tell her the truth?'

He's on his feet, and being helped away by her. So I guess I let go.

'God, whatever,' Jude says. 'You freak.'

When you drive far enough up the mountain, there's almost a little town. I think it's supposed to look Swiss. You'd have to be a kid or really drunk to believe it was even a town, and not just a bunch of restaurants and motels. I guess snow would help. The last time I was here, it was dark and lit up. The buildings looked less like a city, and more like the stars. I wasn't myself, and I knew where to turn. But today there are ten times more roads, and everything looks so unrealistic, and I'm so much more real than I was.

'What did you say?' Pete says. We've figured out who we are, but we're too out of it in different ways to understand.

'I said just keeping talking to me until Jude gets there.'

'What?' he says.

'Forget it. So you're freaking out.'

'We should talk, man,' he says. 'I really want to talk to you about some shit.'

'Go ahead.'

'Don't be mad,' he says. Then nothing happens on his end. He might have just covered the phone with his hand. 'What?'

'I didn't say anything.'

'That fucking cunt,' he says, and maybe laughs. 'I hate that fucking bitch.'

'You're being really vague.'

'She doesn't want me to tell you,' he says. Then nothing happens on his end again.

'Hello?'

'Fuck you, bitch,' he says loudly. 'I don't care.' So I guess she and Jim just arrived, or were already there, and hidden under Pete's hand.

'Put Jude on.'

'It's Larry,' he says, and laughs. Maybe they all laugh together, or else his laugh is so gigantic it echoes all over the cabin.

'I don't understand.'

It's taken me close to an hour of driving around. I kept seeing Pete drunk and still drinking out of a bottle. Sometimes Jude and Jim were partly naked and shot dead beside him. Other times Pete had already raped them before I arrived, so I shot him and sometimes Jude too. Then I'd save Jim from them, and I guess from the more insane part of myself. Sometimes I knew they'd done something before I arrived, so I shot myself. But I couldn't make any idea seem more true, just exciting or not. Right before I pulled up to the cabin and parked, I got stuck for a long time on raping them one at a time on the floor while I yelled things and shot him or her. That one made me pull the gun out from under the seat and start crying so hard that I couldn't get out of the car. I just rolled down the window so they could hear that, and come outside if they wanted to ask me what's wrong. I think that fantasy is the truth, which is why it won't happen, and no one ever comes out.

I heard something in the kitchen. I had the gun out. It took me a while to notice Jude on the floor. This wooden table takes up most of the room, so it's only her legs. I don't care about that.

I only cared about Pete before he turned into a drunk. I didn't even know him back then. That's when I cared about Rand, and Rand wasn't confusing on drugs.

'What happened to you?'

Pete's drinking from a bottle with his shirt off. When he hears my voice, he throws a punch at everything with the hand that is holding the bottle.

'I mean why are you so fucked up? You used to be so different.'

I think he just saw the gun, and then couldn't again, or didn't want to.

'Just tell me what your fucking problem is, okay?'

'Shut up,' he says.

'If you don't, I'll kill you. I really think I will.'

He follows my eyes. I've been looking at his chest. It takes him a while to see it, or maybe think about how it would look in my head. Then he looks at me, and laughs, like he can't believe it's his chest. I guess he doesn't know that I was wondering if I could shoot it.

'Okay, okay,' he says. He takes another drink.

I guess he's crying, not laughing. I didn't realize at first. The other time, he had his back turned to me. So it might just be guilt about Jude. But I don't care anymore if they fucked or she's dead or maybe isn't dead yet.

'I know. You're so confusing. It makes me insane.'

When I put the gun to Pete's neck, he stopped crying and started to walk. I didn't tell him to move. I guess he just thought that's what you do when a gun's at your neck. But he seemed really angry about it. That confused me for a second. By then we'd both come to a stop outside the door to the cabin's only bedroom. Then I guess the gay part of him started to swear at the part of him who isn't.

'Larry,' he says finally.

'I'm thinking.' I look at the gun, then put it into my pocket.

'Don't be mad,' he says. 'I'm just drunk.'

'I don't care.'

'Just don't get mad,' he says, and holds out the bottle. 'You remember that thing about your brother.'

'Yeah, where is he?' I take the bottle.

'Are you still into it?' he says. 'Because I am, if we do it right now.' Then he hits the door angrily or excitedly with his fist. It wasn't clicked shut, and swings open. It's dark inside, and I can hear Jim wake up. I know that gasping sound.

'Wait.' Then I take a huge, huge drink.

I'm pretending Jim's a girl. He just talked, and refocused too much. It might have been the words, more than his voice. I know I said them first. Then I stopped what I was doing, and lay back to watch Jim do gay things to himself.

'Hold me,' Jim says. It's been another minute.

'Okay.' I thought I was holding him already, but I guess it's been more that he was holding onto me while he watched Pete jack off.

'Fuck him,' Pete says. 'Fuck the little bitch.' He's been saying stupid things like that a lot, and making Jim laugh and touch him.

I hold Jim closer, and stroke his head to mean I'm sorry he's so fucked up inside and depressed. That's all I ever did. He did everything else to himself.

'Don't be shy,' Pete says, then laughs, and pushes Jim against me.

'Hey, man.'

'It's okay,' Jim says.

'No, it's not.'

'Come on, Larry,' Pete says, and I guess grabs my hand. It feels like him. I was patting Jim's back.

'What?' I'd closed my eyes. When I open them, I realize what he wants, and that I'm touching Jim's ass. So I close them again. 'No.'

'Bullshit,' Pete says, and holds my hand there.

'It's okay,' Jim says. Then I feel his hand grab whatever's left of my hand, and hold it there too.

'Fucking no.' I yelled that, and yanked.

'Aren't you going to?' Jim says. He sounds so lonely now. I remember. He's trying to help me get off. I can tell it's his hand from the size, and because no one else would care.

'I'm sorry.' Maybe if Jude were here too, it might have helped or else gotten me angry enough.

'It's okay,' Jim says, still trying.

'No, it's not.' It's been so long now, and so much has happened since then, that I guess he forgot how I was.

'Pete, what do I do?'

'I don't fucking know,' he says. He got himself off a while back, and I guess is just sitting there watching us. 'God, you guys make me sick.' Then I hear him stand up.

'Don't go,' Jim says, and I guess looks at Pete.

'Go away, Pete.' Then I hug Jim so he can only see me.

'Shit,' Jim says. I feel him give up, and get upset. I mean I do. But not upset enough to do anything mean to him or cry. It's just him on his own now. I guess I'm still there and perfected in his mind. Maybe that's what I loved.

I just walked out of the bedroom and saw Pete again. Then I wanted to look really close, and pulled out my gun. I guess he'd gotten even more drunk, then passed out halfway through getting dressed. His pants only made it as far as his knees. It's been a minute. There are dents in his face where I was resting the gun, and almost shot. I tested using it like a hammer, but that dent is hidden under his hair. I looked at the fireplace before I did that. I was trying to remember the boy, but there's nothing left there. I had so many reasons to hit Pete or shoot, until I saw the notebook. I guess either Jim or Pete burned it before I got here, and there's a crust. But there were still some great reasons, until I heard something in the kitchen. Then I wasn't sure there were enough yet.

Jude's standing over the sink with a bunched up, wet towel pressed very hard to the back of her head. I think it was white.

'Get that prick out of here,' she says.

'Should I shoot him?'

'I don't care,' she says. 'You're all fucking sick.'

'He raped Jim. So I should shoot him, right?'

She lifts the towel off her head, and looks. There's not even a cloud. So I guess it was pink to begin with, and she was faking. 'Your brother hit me on the head, you know,' she says.

'Bullshit.'

'Fuck all of you,' she says.

'Anyway, you're okay.'

Jim was sitting crosslegged on the bed. I guess he got depressed before he saw me, and I didn't help. When he looks this depressed, you can move him around like a blind guy, if you're careful.

'You hit her.' I have him by arms. We're in the kitchen now.

'Not on purpose,' he says.

'Why?'

'I was trying to hit Pete,' he says.

Now Jude's eyes are trying to remember and figure that out. 'No, he wasn't,' she says afterwards.

'Just tell the fucking truth, Jim.'

'He was going to beat her up,' he says.

'That's not true,' Jude says to him, then looks angrily at me. 'He was being all faggy with Pete. It was sick.'

'No, I wasn't,' Jim says.

I used to know everything in Jim's eyes. I haven't been able to look at them deeply for a year. I dreamed about doing that again. When he was depressed, they were the reason I didn't love him every minute. So they're just unbelieveably important.

'Look at me.' He hasn't, or won't.

He looks at Jude instead. I don't know why, but that does it. 'You don't love me.' Then I hit him as hard as I can in the face.

I have my eyes closed. Jim's pelvic bones are stabbing into my ass. I guess I knocked him to the floor, and sat down on his stomach. We're both very thin everywhere, and have dramatic, large hips. Mine used to hurt girls, and now I know what they felt. It's just that Jim's aren't moving. It's been a while since I punched him so hard that I doubt I could have seen anything about me in his eyes if I looked.

'Pete.' That was a loud yell.

I hear someone touch or lean against the closed door, but not push it open.

'Jude?'

He or she opens the door, and walks closer to me. Then whoever's knees crack. So it's probably her. I'm sure he'd just stand there all drunk.

'Do you think he'll still hear me?'

'He's not dead, Larry,' she says, I guess angrily. That took her a second. So she could have easily thought up a lie. Then she raises her voice. 'Pete.'

I hear the door open again, and smell Pete.

'What the fuck?' he says, and I think starts to leave from the sound of the door.

'Tell him for fuck's sake,' she says.

'What should I say?' I mean to Jim.

'Fuck, I don't know. That you're sorry?' she says, and raises her voice. 'Tell him, Pete. Jesus Christ, you asshole.'

Then I think and think. 'That's not enough.'

I'm in the cabin's livingroom with Pete. He's out of beer, and lying back on the couch all upset about that. First I climbed off Jim. Then Jude helped him stand up. I know I hit him harder than I hit the boy, but he can still talk to her. So I came out here and asked Pete what he was going to tell me those times if it wasn't that he loved me. That's what's been happening. He's still telling me he doesn't. I'm just not listening now because he's moved on to something gay that explains Gilman's thing with the boy. I don't care at this point. When I climbed off the boy, and walked into the woods, he wasn't dead yet. That's the thing. So Pete strangled him to death. The boy even begged Jude to stop Pete, but I guess she loved Pete and wouldn't. So I've been telling the truth, and the world was the lie. Or it feels like that now. Maybe when I'm dead, I'll make sense. Or I'll destroy everyone who's alive and loved me like Rand did.

I'm out in the woods with a shovel and this gigantic trash bag I found under the sink. It rained, and the sloppy ground's hard to control. I don't even hear someone walk through the woods, then stand around watching me dig for a while. It takes his raspy cough. That's my fault.

I stop digging, and look in the hole. It wouldn't be him if the black, twisted shape wasn't wearing black parts of his shoes. 'So, yeah.'

I guess Jim doesn't know what to say.

'What do you want?' Then I start digging around him again, even though the hole's basically a hole. It's time to turn the shovel over, and use it on him like an axe.

'I can't believe it,' Jim says.

'Me neither.' Then I hit him as hard as I can on the knees. They take three swings to break, and not just rock from side to side.

'I won't say anything,' Jim says.

'Thanks. I won't either.' I'm just chopping the body all over. I don't care.

Jim helped me lift the heavy bag into the trunk. After that he felt so weak, I helped him walk. We just drove off. I'm watching the side of the road for that trail. I think we already passed it. The part of me that hasn't slept for three days has gotten really important. Jim tuned the car radio to his station as soon as we left. From his face, you'd think it was the news on a terrible day. I guess that's the lyrics, and what I did. They're all about being in love, no matter who's singing them or whatever music is barely playing around them. I don't know what else.

'It doesn't matter.' Those are my lyrics. I guess those songs or what I know has made me sad about everything I'll never know. So that's my music.

'I know,' he says.

'I guess we're even.'

'There,' he says.

'There, what?' I look where he's looking. It's a cliff. If I was with anyone other than him, I'd drive off it. I'm tired enough. Or I'd tell him or her to get out first. I know that's not what he means. He's just trying to help.

'Yeah, that'll work.'

5

I was used to Jim's face, and numbed by my hours around it. I guess he got uglier on the drive, and Mom's scared. I look out of it, too. Dad seems confused by my mom, or sees Jim in some way I don't get. She stands up drunkenly, but Dad can't. He might be trying.

'Where have you been?' she says, standing there. It's just her and a drink.

'Hiking.'

Jim's looking at her through his fingers. His shirt's torn and dirty, too.

'Jimmy?' she says.

'He got hurt. He fell.'

Jim's suddenly crying so hard, he can't stand very well. We're all just watching him waver around, and he's looking at her.

'Call the police.' I just punched him in the shoulder, then realized what I'd done or could do.

'No, don't,' Jim says, and looks at me.

I guess my dad still knows something about the police, because he moves around scarily in his chair.

'Call the fucking police.'

'Please don't, please,' Jim says.

'Jimmy?' my mom says.

I grab Jim by the shoulders and walk him and me to the couch. He stumbles a few times, but I feel weirdly strong. I sit both of us down. My mom sat down too. I didn't see it happen. She looks at my dad's face. There's just a trace of him left in what's mostly a skull. I want to tell him the truth, but it won't understand. I think that's what's going on. So I look at it, and concentrate.

'I killed his friend Bill, okay?'

That takes everyone a second. 'Honey,' my mom says. 'You didn't kill Rand.'

'I know.'

'You just think you did,' she says.

'No, I killed his friend Bill. I killed him, okay? I fucking killed him.'

My mom looks drunkenly at Jim, but I can't take my eyes off my dad because I'll kill them or me. I just miss him so much, and Rand. It's pathetic.

'Dad, I'm fucking insane.'

'Your dad doesn't understand,' my mom says.

'It was an accident,' Jim says.

'It was so not an accident.'

'Yeah, it was,' Jim says. 'Jude told me.'

'Jude?' my mom says.

'Larry got mad at Bill and started hitting him,' Jim says. 'Then this other friend of Larry's killed Bill.'

The coffee table has magazines on it, and all her drinking glasses from today. I kick it, and everything either slides off or rolls around wildly. Then I grab the table by the edge, and stand up. I throw it at the wall. It doesn't get that far and falls down on its side. I lost my dad's eyes when I threw it.

'Call the police.'

'Sit down,' my mom says.

'No, listen.' I screamed that. 'Dad, fuck, come on.'

Jim grabs my leg from behind, and rubs it. So I close my eyes, and try hard to think about what that could mean. Then I realize he's just tugging on my pants so I'll sit.

'Please call the police.'

'We're not going to call the police,' my mom says. 'I'll call Dr. Thorne.'

'Sit down, Larry,' my dad says. That was really close to his old, angry voice. So I guess we're all shocked.

I sat down. I didn't notice when I did. I can't think, but I can tell Jim is rubbing my back. It has to mean something. 'Okay.' Then I start rubbing his too.

Mom's on the phone. My dad looks like he's forgotten that something is wrong. He's turned slightly the other way in his chair, I guess so he can look at whatever's on TV right now. It's too flat to think about. Jim has his arm around me, and is watching TV too. It's some woman singing.

'Just a minute,' my mom says, and hands me the phone. That makes Jim look at me, and something happen in his arm.

'Yeah.'

'Tell me what's wrong,' says Dr. Thorne's voice. It's flat, too.

'I killed someone.'

'What does that mean?' his voice says.

'I beat a friend of Jim's to death.'

'Are you sure?' his voice says.

'No.'

'Okay,' his voice says. Then I guess he decides what to ask. So I look at my mom. It felt important. I don't know what I thought I could see, or what difference it would make if it looked like she loved me. But she doesn't, or I'd know.

'I want them to call the police.'

'Why don't we talk some more first,' his voice says.

'About what?'

'I'm not sure that you know what you've done, and what you haven't done,' his voice says.

'Right now I do. I can't explain it.'

'How do you know?' his voice says. 'You blame yourself for things you haven't done, and deny responsibility for things you have done.'

'Not right now.'

He doesn't say anything, but I know what he's thinking. It's the usual deep, unfriendly silence he always uses with me.

'I know what I did to Jim.'

'Let me talk to him,' Jim says immediately. His arm's also gone, or I can't feel it.

'What did you do?' his voice says.

That takes me a second. 'My mom's sitting here.'

'Let me talk to him,' Jim says more loudly.

'Allright,' his voice says. 'Let me talk to Jim.'

'No.'

'Larry,' Jim says. 'Come on.'

'Come on, what?'

'Larry,' says his voice.

'What?'

'Listen to me,' his voice says. 'Just listen. Your brother is very, very fragile. He has a very serious emotional disorder. Do you understand?'

'So do I.'

'Please just put him on the phone,' his voice says. 'Then we'll talk.'

'Shit.' I hand the phone to Jim. I don't know why I ever thought I could be as importantly fucked up as Jim.

*   *   *

I walked out of the room. I leaned on the railing that goes up the side of the stairs and tried to think. Jim's still talking to Dr. Thorne and sometimes to my mom, or she'll talk to him. Everyone I can hear sounds so relaxed without me, or depressed about who I am now, or was, or never was. My dad might not care. It just doesn't make any sense. I guess that's why I've started shaking so hard, I have to hit the railing over and over to think. It hasn't helped yet, and either no one can hear the dull sound that makes or else cares why I would make it.

I just shot my mom and dad. I did her from the door, then walked over to him. I might have shot her again on the way. He was watching TV. I don't know about her. Jim's sitting very still on the couch with the phone to his ear. He wasn't the point until they were shot. Then I aimed at him. He was looking at my mom, not me. That made me want to shoot, but I didn't. Then I guess nothing happened until I realized what did, and looked at my parents. Jim's still looking at her. She'd be looking back at him, if she could see. I think I'm telling him to stop looking at her, but he won't. Then I guess I hit him in the shoulder to knock his eyes loose.

'Hello.' Jim's pinned face down on the couch by his neck. He can't see her. I'm just finding what's left on the phone. It's been a minute, and I don't expect much.

'Hello,' says Dr. Thorne's voice. It's still exactly flat.

'Yeah.'

'Larry,' his voice says. 'Tell me what just happened.'

'You wouldn't understand.'

'Let me talk to Jim again,' his voice says.

'Okay.' I hold the phone to Jim's head, and ease up on his neck. He tries to say something, but can't. So I let go completely. 'Say whatever you want.'

'Hello?' Jim says. That sounded bad. So I guess he rubs his throat gently to help.

I'd put the gun back in my pocket at some point. But I pull it out, and let it hang at my side. When Jim sees it, he hides almost all of his face under a pillow near his head.

'No.' I kick the couch.

'It's okay,' Jim says to one of us.

'Jim.' I just turned the gun on myself. It's very hard. He can't see, so I have to scream his name again.

There he is. 'It's okay,' he says to Dr. Thorne. So I guess he thinks it is.

'No, it's not.'

'What?' Jim says. He stops rubbing his neck and holds out one of his arms. I can't figure that out, unless he wants the gun. So I throw it as hard as I can across the room. It hits the wall behind my mom.

'Oh, God.'

'Okay,' Jim says to Dr. Thorne. 'Bye.' He's still reaching for me, even after he clicks off the phone.

'What.' I looked at his hand, and just screamed that.

I couldn't think, so Jim did. I limped upstairs behind him, or must have. He helped me lie down on my bed. It's nothing gay. We're just lying here dressed, side by side like two friends. It got darker outside, and that had this effect I always liked on my room. After a while, I wanted to see Jim again. I hadn't for maybe an hour. He's just been daydreaming, I guess on his back, but looked over at me. Then we thought for a while, probably about each other. I definitely thought about him.

'I'm sorry, Jim.' I was waiting for it to grow darker. He's barely there now.

That takes him a second. 'Are you okay?' he says.

'Yeah.'

'That's good,' he says.

'I know what I did to you, and I'm sorry. I thought you were like me.'

'That's okay,' he says.

'I feel really bad.'

'I think about Rand all the time,' he says. 'That's what's hard.'

'You probably hate me.'

'No,' he says, and I think turns over onto his side. He must be facing away. So I guess he does, and can't admit it.

'Can I ask you something?' I wanted to say something else.

'What?' he says. He's facing me. I can smell it. Maybe he never turned over at all. So maybe it isn't just hate. Then I think suddenly about my hands. He's so close, and they're doing nothing important on my chest.

'Just about Rand.'

'He was a strange guy,' he says.

'I thought he had sex with you.'

'I wanted to,' Jim says. 'But he would only take pictures.'

'That's my fault.'

'So were you in love with him?' Jim says.

'No, he just confused me.'

'I sort of loved him, but he loved you,' Jim says. 'It was hard.'

'I don't want to think about that.'

'Okay,' Jim says. 'I just hated that he loved you.'

'I really love Jude.'

'She seems nice,' he says.

'God, I'm so sorry.'

'I think maybe you were insane,' he says.

'Yeah, I don't know why.'

'I just don't know what's going to happen,' he says.

'I guess you'll live with Aunt Elaine.'

'No, you know what I mean,' he says.

That takes me a second. It also takes feeling his hand on my arm. He lets it rest for a second, then rubs. We were always like this, but the world was okay and still waiting for us. 'What do you want to happen?'

'I don't know,' he says.

'Me, neither.'

Jim fell asleep, but I couldn't. I guess he was waiting for me to decide. But I was waiting for him. There's a tiny yellow light aimed at the most barren spot on my desk. It's from a weird, bendable lamp I bought. I was writing a note to Jim, then couldn't finish. I don't know what made me stop, and come downstairs instead. It might have been watching him lie there without me. I took some bedsheets out of the hall closet first. I unfolded one, and walked into the living room, holding it in front of me by the edges. I got it thrown over my dad, then adjusted it so he was gone. My mom was harder. When I knelt down to fix my dad's sheet, my stupid leg started hurting again. I missed her, then had to pick it back up with my eyes closed. She's gone now. The livingroom smells like a gun has gone off, and the whole thing with them and my leg has made me even more tired. I just sat down, and found the phone. It had slipped between the cushions, or was hidden there by Jim. I couldn't think of anyone to call until I remembered a loose paper scrap in my pocket.

'Did it work?' I just said who I was. I'm sure I sound different. The Franks hadn't woken up yet, but he's starting to figure me out.

'What the hell?' he says.

'We'll talk to you in the morning,' Mrs. Frank says. I guess she took the phone away from him, or leaned in.

'No.'

'Excuse me?' she says.

'I really need to hear what he said.' I didn't realize I did until she told me I couldn't.

'We'll call you first thing,' she says.

'I have to hear it.'

'It's fine, Wayne,' she says to him. 'What kind of computer do you have?'

'I don't know. A Mac.'

'Can you download MP3s?' she says.

'I'll figure it out.'

'You either need Real Audio or . . .' she says, or starts.

'Whatever, yeah.' It's too complicated. So I hang up to stop it.

You can easily sneak into Gilman's backyard, if you're quiet. You just have to push through some bushes. The only hard thing is avoiding the million dead leaves. His window is three of them down. It's the blackest one. So it's harder to tap on quietly than I thought. I know it's just paint.

'It's Larry.'

Gilman mumbles a word. It was almost like something a dead guy might say. I mean I don't understand. So I tap the glass harder. Then there's an underwear-brushed-across-skin kind of sound, and some creaks.

'I killed my parents.'

The window cracks open an inch. Even that took him a second of probably looking at me. 'What do you want?' his voice says quietly.

'I don't know.'

'That fucking bug,' his voice says. So I guess he didn't hear, or else couldn't care less if he did.

'I killed my parents.'

'Wait a second,' his voice says. Then nothing happens. The blackness in there is adjusting to me. It's just really dark, and he's not wearing a shirt or much else. He's massively thin and white, and almost everything that made him seem evil to me has been taken or ripped off his walls.

'Just talk to me.'

'Fucking asshole,' he says.

'What's the matter?' I can almost see his eyes.

'Nothing,' he says.

'Can I come in?' I just cupped my eyes, then put my face close to the window. Everything's so torn up.

'No,' he says.

'Then you come out.'

There he is completely. He's hugging himself, and just wearing underwear like I thought. They're still bent out of shape from some exciting idea he was having or dreamed, and I haven't ruined that. So I'm confused. There's just nothing else to look at in there. So I don't care what he thinks.

'I won't kill you.'

Their backyard's big enough for a rectangular pool. There's even a stylized wood shack on one side where you can watch people swim without getting too sunburned. It's still dark. He wanted to sit there, I guess out of habit. I don't know why I care. I keep thinking about what I saw in his room. It was either sit quietly by the pool, or drive up to the hill and say whatever we want. I threw that out there. He said no, but I can tell he's not completely decided. I just threw out the idea of taking Pete too. That did something I might understand to his eyes, and probably something to mine that I don't.

'Did you love him or something?' It's been a few minutes.
    'Who?' he says. He was looking emotionally at the pool, but now he's looking at me like I'm the pool. I think he's just confused about 'did.' We're relaxed in two metal chairs. 'Oh, fuck, no.'
    'Then why did you want us to kill him?'
    'I don't know,' he says. 'Maybe I hate gay people.'
    'They're confusing.'
    'No, they're not,' he says.
    'I think they are.'
    'I always admired that you killed that guy Rand,' he says. 'Maybe that's why.'
    'I don't want to talk about that.'
    'Yeah, well, I just thought it was cool,' he says.
    'Sometimes I think I want people to like me so much that I don't care if they're gay, and want me to be gay.'
    'I don't think about things like that,' he says, and sits up. He folds his hands, or one grabs the other for help.
    'Yeah, you do.'
    He doesn't say anything for so long that I give him a look. He closed his eyes at some point in all that, I don't know when. Maybe when he sat up.
    'Yeah, you do.'
    'I just don't want anyone to know me,' he says.
    'Why? You're cool.'
    'Yeah?' he says. 'When did you decide that?'
    I have to think. 'Honestly?'
    'No,' he says, and looks at me. 'I'm fucking dead.' It took him a second. 'That fucking bug told the police I raped him.'
    'I'm dead, too.'

'You really are,' he says. He smiles, then tries not to again. It's nice. 'Okay, so when did you decide?'

We just talked for a while. I guess I mostly asked personal questions. He was silent a lot. Then he went back in the house, and came out with his phone. He was leaving a really long message for Jeanne. When he talks to other Nazis, even her, you'd never think he was lonely. I just said that, which made him forget what he was saying to Jeanne for a second. I know that's mean. His message was mostly an order to put certain guns in her car trunk, then meet with the rest of their group at some place with a name I don't know. It might be made up. First he gave me a dirty, folded piece of paper. He turned on the pool's underwater floodlights, so I could read it. I'm on my knees, holding it about an inch off the surface. I expected something private and gay, but it's just an old, printed out list of the students he's wanted to shoot. Tran isn't on it. I read it three times to make sure, then checked in on Gilman. I'm sure I looked confused. He's off the phone now, and was watching me read. The names on the list are almost three-quarters girls', and the words all sound white. He looks lonely again. I think that's partly some thought about me, and partly about maybe shooting himself afterwards like the Columbine guys. That's part of what we were talking about. He doesn't really want to die, I can tell. He's like me. I think he almost asked me to be there and shoot him. He'll probably ask Jeanne, or another Nazi if I don't. Before I decide, I need to know if I can get that upset. I just threw out the hill and maybe Pete combination again, then asked to use the phone while he decided. He handed it to me, then started crying. He's trying to be really quiet about that, I guess so his parents won't hear.

*   *   *

'Where are you?' Jim says. I was standing by the fence when he answered. Now I'm walking crazedly in a circle. I don't know why I keep looking at Gilman. I guess it's because he keeps crying and looking at me.

'I thought you were okay.'

'Why did you leave me here?' he says. He was already out of breath. I guess he's crying now too.

'You need to take your pills.'

'They're downstairs,' he says or yells. 'I'm not going down there.'

'I'll come back.' I guess I stupidly felt like what I did at the house had gone somewhere I couldn't.

'When?' he says.

'Wait for me out front, and I'll pick you up.'

'No,' he says.

'Just close your eyes, and go outside.'

'I can't,' he says.

'I covered them up with sheets.'

'I can't,' he says more loudly.

Gilman's still crying and looking at me when he can, but that's only his problem. When Jim cries, he always ruins me. I forget that. It's probably why I either love him too much or not enough, and not anyone else. I don't know. It just makes Gilman seem like he'd be simple to love or kill. I know he's not.

'Don't go to school today.' Jude picked up the phone when she heard me. I can tell she was sleeping. It means something. First I sat down next to Gilman, and looked at him intensely until he tried to look at me intensely, then couldn't. That does too.

'Larry?' Jude's voice says again.

'Just don't.'

'Okay,' Gilman says in this squeaky and sniffling voice.

'Why don't you come over?' her voice says. That would have sounded so soft even two days ago.

'I'm insane, Jude.' Then I put my hand over the phone. 'With Pete or without?'

'Come over, okay?' her voice says.

I take my hand off the phone. 'Don't go to school today.' Then I put it back on.

'Okay, okay,' her voice says.

'Without,' Gilman says, and kind of slaps both his hands over his face.

I take my hand off the phone for a second. 'I need to do something, and then I'll maybe come over.'

'Larry,' Gilman says.

'Hold on for a second.' Then I cover the phone. 'What?'

'I mean without you,' Gilman says.

'I'm really stupid, Larry,' her voice says.

'Bullshit.' Then I uncover the phone. 'It so doesn't matter, Jude.'

You can tell Gilman cried and could start up again. It's deep in his eyes. They're usually too cold. I don't care why anymore. I left the folded piece of paper by the pool. I thought he was staring at it. When I picked it up, I realized he was staring at the pool. He's turned off the lights, I guess to hide that he'd been crying. So the pool's just a picture of the sky, which means the stars and a few blurry inches of trees.

'Here.' I held out the paper. I shook it around.

'Thanks,' he says, then slowly takes it.

'So why them?'

'I think we voted,' he says. 'I don't know. It was like a year ago.'

'Yeah, because Tran's not on it.'

'It was just people we didn't know,' he says. 'It's pathetic.'

'So it's good you aren't going to do it.'

'Yeah,' he says. 'I just want to kill Pete. I hate his fucking bullshit.'

'You will. It'll be great.'

'Yeah?' he says. He sits forward. His eyes aren't feeling anything bad or critical about me, or I can't see it. He also just looks really thin and not German and not anything else he wants to be. 'I don't give a fuck.'

'Yeah, you do.'

Gilman looks at the stars. I mean the ones that are upside down and backwards and wavering a little on the pool. So I look at them too. 'I'm not gay,' he says finally. 'I'm sorry.'

'I know. You're just in love with Pete.'

'No, I'm not,' he says. 'I hate him.'

'Look, I had sex with my brother. That doesn't mean I'm gay.'

'Yeah, it does,' he says.

Then we sit quietly for a while. I guess I look at him sometimes, and he looks at the pool. I don't why I thought he would care.

'You know that thing about Dylan Kliebald?' he says finally, and stands up. So I guess he just wants me to leave. 'And how he supposedly did all that shit because he couldn't have Harris?'

'He wasn't gay.'

'I know, so maybe you're like that,' he says. Then he starts to walk back towards the house without me.

'God, I wish.'

When I get home, I just sit in the car for a minute. It's light. I think I would have driven away, if I didn't look up and see Jim in my window. I guess he's been watching for me. After he's cried for a while, he looks more like my mom than himself. I always look more or less like my dad. Seeing her face used to stop me, if I hadn't already stopped on my own. I couldn't figure that out, and can't now. If it was one of those times when I felt sorry for him, or was afraid I was gay, I'd decide I was sick and not in love with anyone. Jim just waved, so I guess I was smiling at some idea I used to have about Mom, and he misunderstood. Now I'm not.

Jim just took his medication. It seemed like a huge group of pills. I got the bottles for him out of the bathroom downstairs. He's lying quietly on my bed, I guess to let everything sink in or spread. I'm online, just to be somewhere else. That means I'm sitting at my desk. I saw the Franks' emails, then took the framed picture of Rand off my dresser. It's propped up near my mouse where I can see him again if I want.

'Dr. Thorne called,' Jim says. He sounds spacier already.

'Yeah.'

'He wanted us to come in today,' he says, and laughs.

'We should.' I laughed too.

'I think it's starting to hit me,' he says.

'Yeah, I know. Wait a minute.'

'It's fake,' Jim says. It was more like a whisper. I just played the two MP3s a lot. After a while, I was clicking and clicking.

'I know.'

They're just these two eerie, several seconds long sounds unless you crank it. I might have thought they were real, if I hadn't killed my parents. I can't explain that. When you turn the sound up until it almost distorts, you can hear these weakened voices. They're so hard to figure out that I guess they sounded dead to me once.

'I can't find any,' I think one voice says. It's not even a man's.

Maybe it's what Rand's soul sounded like, but I'm not gay, and never was, and can't tell.

'He never sounded like that, did he?'

'It's fake,' Jim says again. He doesn't sound like himself, either. So I don't know.

'I'm over here,' I think the second voice says. It's almost for sure an old man's. When I used to hear fake recordings of no one I knew, I felt something. I guess the voices always sounded old. Maybe that's all I felt.

'She told me they were fake,' I think Jim says.

'Who?'

'That reporter,' I think Jim says.

'Yeah?' I don't care about her anymore. Or Rand either, I guess. The picture of him is so flat. It used to be like looking into a tunnel.

I had to walk Jim carefully down the stairs from behind while he covered his eyes. I wasn't going to look at my parents until I heard something I used to like. The TV's still on. I think if it was off, they'd be too dead. I guess it's a thing on some morning news show about Marilyn Manson. I liked him before Rand died. Everyone I knew sort of did. Actually, I think he wore off before that. I only looked at the TV to see if he'd changed. He was wearing his makeup and costume from years back, or ones just like that. I bet Gilman still listens deeply to him. That's all I thought. Nothing about my parents being dead, or how he used to upset them. I think if people understood why Marilyn Manson wears off, they'd like Gilman for being so confused and gullible about death. I liked him more when I thought that, but not enough to care if he kills Pete or not, then himself. I know that's cold. So maybe I looked at where they used to be too. I mean my parents. I didn't feel like I did. But I can't believe Marilyn

Manson would make me think about death after everything that's really happened.

We just drove up in front of Jim's school. It was sort of automatic for me. I know how terrible he looks. He'd been spaced out on medication and maybe the road. He looked at the school, or at the kids roughly his age being dropped off in front. I guess he doesn't want to get out, and I don't think I would have let him. When I saw all those kids, and realized how much he wasn't like them, I was going to tell him I love him. I just couldn't or don't. Then that teacher Jim likes put his face in the window. I hadn't seen him. He smiles at Jim like nothing's wrong, even though Jim is unbelievably bruised and swollen up from being beaten.

'We missed you yesterday,' the teacher says. He's a little heavyset and blond and just a nothing looking man.

'Hi,' Jim says quietly.

The teacher keeps smiling at Jim, then smiles at me too. 'Are you the famous Larry?' he says.

'Yeah.'

Something's happened to his smile. I think it's almost a laugh. 'Okay,' he says. Then he squeezes Jim's shoulder and walks off. Jim turns, and watches him go. When he's a distance away, he looks back at Jim again without the smile.

That takes me a second. 'Maybe you can live with him.' I meant that as a joke, but I guess it isn't.

'I'm sure he'd let me,' Jim says.

I don't know why, but I lose it. I shove Jim as hard as I can against the passenger door. It wasn't very hard. First I looked out, and saw that teacher walking back toward my car with another angry looking adult. But that wasn't it.

'Get out, okay?'

'You don't mind?' Jim says. I do, but he's already out, or almost. He just has to slam the door.

'I don't know.'

It only takes a few minutes to drive from his school to the high school. But there was time to decide how I'd finish that note I was writing to Jim, if he cared at this point. I guess I'd write that when I was his age, Dad got cancer and grew so confusing it made our mom into a drunk. I didn't know the only person who loved me back then was taking naked pictures of Jim. Jim should have told me. Or Rand should have loved me enough not to start. Maybe Jim seemed so depressed that Rand thought it wouldn't matter. Or Rand was so upset about me, he didn't care. But Jim would get confused late at night without telling me why and want to talk. Words used to interest me, but I guess he just wanted the love. So I pretended with him. I didn't know he loved Rand, and was pretending with me. Maybe if I'd realized that, I wouldn't have pretended. Maybe Rand knew I would love him too much, and thought Jim was like him. I mean so depressed all the time he couldn't really love anyone. But Jim could, and I couldn't. I don't know what made us not love one another. I just know that what we did or didn't do in those days is what made me insane. I don't know about them. I think if I could write all that down, Jim would understand why I don't love him, if he cares. Then I could kill myself. But I'm sure it would only make him miss Rand, and want to kill himself again, so I won't.

'Hey.' I just sat down next to Will on the grass. It's like a little park between the school and a circular driveway we try not to face. It was always too intense. Buses drive in and drop students off, then pick them up later, I guess. You can watch them stand around and wake up. People pause their cars there for a second, if they're parents.

'What's up?' Will says in this voice like he doesn't care what I say next. I guess he was always like that.

'Nothing. Where's Tran?'

'Somewhere being a freak,' he says.

Then we just sit there and watch how the world works against us like always.

'You want to know something?'

'Not really,' Will says.

I don't care if he does. Maybe most friends don't. Maybe it's not that important. So I suddenly have a nice second or two of realizing we're friends, and actually look at him. I know I always do. 'Wow.'

'What?' he says, and looks back at me.

'I'm sorry about stealing Jude from you.'

'Okay,' he says.

'You're a really good friend.'

'Yeah, well, you suck,' he says, and smiles. When he does that, he has to look away at nothing. I checked. I don't know why it's so nice. It's still nice when I see the parked car. I didn't notice it there until Gilman got out by himself with a gun. I didn't recognize the gun until everyone looked at the circular driveway like it was incredibly confusing. Then I'm just surprised it's only Gilman, and that he didn't kill Pete, or killing Pete didn't help.

'Oh, Jesus,' Will says.

Gilman shoots in front of him. That's the first thing. His gun was aimed at a small crowd of guys who start crouching or moving around. I think he got a girl. Then I can't see anything because the people between us are running. There he barely is. He stopped walking. I think he's trying to see who he's shooting. Then he walks slowly into the school. He's gone. Everyone around us sits down again, laughing nervously and talking. I don't really know them. Will just started talking to them and other people we don't even like. I think a few of them are crying. I keep thinking Gilman stopped, or was tackled and stopped by someone. Then I'll hear another shot. They've gotten weirdly far apart. So I guess he finally cares about who's getting killed. Maybe they're even people he knows. Eventually the shooting just ends. Maybe when he started to care who was dead, he realized he could die. Or he finally figured out what he wanted to do, and either did it or knew that he couldn't. Maybe the last shot was aimed at himself. It sounded like all the others.